Claimed in Alaska

Lillith Carrie

BOLD BOOKS
PUBLISHING

© Copyright 2024 - Lillith Carrie All rights reserved.

It is not legal to reproduce, duplicate, or transmit any part of this document in either electronic means or in printed format. Recording of this publication is strictly prohibited and any storage of this document is not allowed unless with written permission from the publisher except for the use of brief quotations in a book review.

This book is a work of fiction. Any resemblance to persons, living or dead, or places, events or locations is purely coincidental.

All rights reserved. This book or any portion thereof may not be reproduced or used in any manner whatsoever without the express written permission of the publisher except for the use of brief quotations in a book review.

Cover Design by Elizabeth F. an exclusive designer with Bold Books Publishing

Edited by Aimee Ferro Edits

In collaboration with Bold Books Publishing

Printed in the United States

First edition, 2024.

www.lillithcarriepublishing.com

To the rugged men of Alaska,
Who heat up the cold nights with firey passion,
And leave their mark on the untouched snow.

Chapter 1

Wolves, My Ass

Lucy

"Just up this hill, ma'am, and we should be able to see the cabin." My trail guide motions toward the seemingly endless slope in front of us. Fuck. That isn't a hill, it's a damn mountain. The guide is your typical Alaskan mountain man, full on beard, fur hat with a lumberjack physique. I feel woefully under-prepared and very, *very* cold in my jeans, boots, puffer jacket, and beanie.

"Please, call me Lucy." The sound of the snow crunching under our snowshoes grates against the peaceful silence of the snow-covered hillside. I suppose it's lucky that the airport we flew into had one pair left for sale.

It wasn't so much an airport as much as it was a single shack with a runway and a single plane for hire. The fact that I not only had to hire a seaplane to Telkeetna to get here, but I also needed snowshoes to make it to my father's cabin made me question, not for the first time, what the hell I had gotten myself into.

Then again, what was I expecting when I turned down my father's solicitor's offer to place the cabin on the market for me, opting to fly into Anchorage, Alaska myself when I had never even gone on so much as a small hike before this?

It seemed like the better option was to come see the property for myself so I could make an informed decision. Did I want to sell the home my estranged father used as a hiding place for the last fifteen years, or did I want to see the place myself and maybe burn it down?

While burning down seemed unlikely in this cold of weather, I can't push the sentiment entirely from my mind.

After I graduated from Brown University with a degree in Literature, I moved in with a roommate last spring, who I knew through a friend of a friend. Before I knew it, six months had gone by, I still didn't have a job, and the inheritance from my grandparents was running out. To top it all off, last week the landlord came pounding on our front door demanding rent.

Apparently, my roommate, who I had been giving my rent money to, stopped paying the damn rent after about two months. She said she was going on vacation, and I still haven't heard from her.

So there I was, getting kicked out of my apartment when the solicitor showed up on my doorstep, telling me my father, Simon, died, and he left everything to me...well, if a cabin in the middle of nowhere Alaska and a checking account with $17 can be considered *everything*.

Talk about a bad situation having a silver lining. *Sort of.*

When I got the news that Simon had passed, I didn't really feel anything. Hell, I was more upset about the money my roommate scammed from me. But it wasn't like I knew the guy.

Asshole upped and left when I was seven years old, sending a birthday card every other year.

Shit. He didn't even come to get me after Mom died five years later. Instead, I had to go live with my grandparents. Not that it was a bad thing...they took care of me well enough.

Damn, climbing this hill is hard.

Regardless of how I feel, my guide, who I've taken to calling "Lumberjack" in my head, is barely out of breath. While I on the other hand feel like I'm dying. Approaching the top of the hill, I sigh with relief. Small white puffs of cold air escape my lips every time I breathe out reminding me of just how fucking cold this place is.

"I've never worn snowshoes before," I admit, as if that's why I'm having such a hard time.

"Oh, no, ma'am, you're a natural." Lumberjack is a terrible liar, and based on his expression I can tell he knows it too. We both ignore the blatant lie, continuing in silence even though I internally grate at the use of the honorific instead of my name.

Maybe if I pelt him with a snowball, he'll stop calling me 'ma'am'.

In awkward silence, we finally round the top of the hill. The cabin is in view, maybe 300 yards ahead of me, when the sight of paw prints in the snow stops me in my tracks.

"Uh...is that...is that a common occurrence?" I ask, swallowing nervously.

"The snow, ma'am?" Lumberjack chuckles as he continues walking, "yes, very common."

Smartass.

My eyes roll so hard I almost see the back of my head. "No, not the snow." Despite the boldness in my voice, I can't stop my finger from shaking slightly as I point at the tracks. "The paw prints. What kind of animal made that? A fucking polar bear?"

Lumberjack stops, his eyes widening, as he turns and walks back toward me, squatting down near the prints. "No, ma'am, those look to be more like wolves. Probably just passin' through. Nothin' to worry about."

I swear to god, if he calls me ma'am one more time...

His voice is reluctant, his eyes darting around us as he speaks again, "though, these are the biggest wolf prints I've seen." He reaches to touch one, then quickly withdraws, shaking his head. Standing, all worry seems to have melted from his face. "But, as I said before, probably just passin' through." He continues walking as if didn't just kind of admit that there are giant wolves possibly roaming the area.

My heart races as my eyes linger on the tracks for a moment longer. Wolves, my ass. If wolves made those tracks, they had to be on...steroids. Or something. Despite being aware that I know next to nothing about animals or the Alaskan wilderness, I can't help but scan the treeline for the owners of the overly large paw prints, just in case Lumberjack is wrong as well.

It's times like these where I wonder what use my literary degree is if I might just end up in the belly of some feral wolf anyway. Or a bear. Bears are out here too, right? Out of the places my thoughtless, selfish, deserting sperm donor could have settled, why the fuck did it have to be the Alaskan wilderness?

With all the courage I can muster, I force my body to put one foot in front of the other to continue my trek behind him, hoping that I'm not being led to my eventual demise by feral wolves and that I'm least somewhat safe with this mountain of a man. My brow furrows as I observe the sun low on the horizon. It can't be later than 3pm, but the sun is already setting?

"It's getting dark already?" I comment, watching my guide's head nod from in front of me.

"Yes, there isn't much sunlight this time of year."

Right. I remember before I left I read about how Alaska's location on the Earth gave it either really long or really short days, depending on the time of the year. I guess reading about it I didn't get the full idea, but seeing it in person—it's definitely something.

By the time we reach the crest of the hill, I'm not breathing as bad as I was when I was walking up the damn thing. Despite my improvement, though, I'm still about ten times more haggard than Lumberjack, who has probably spent his entire life in this climate since trekking through snowy hills seems to be no more difficult to him than a walk in the park. He saunters across the snow as if it's the most natural thing in the world.

As much as I hate to admit it, I wouldn't have made it out here without him. However, his invaluable assistance through this journey doesn't stop me from wanting to slap that smirk off his face when he turns to meet my exhausted gaze. He even slightly chuckles as I struggle the rest of the way to the front door through the snow. Though, he tries to cover it with a cough when I glare at him.

Finally reaching the front door, my gloves fumble in my jacket pocket for the keys to the cabin. I pull them triumphantly from my pocket only to realize...it's my lighter.

"Hold on, I have the keys somewhere," I reply, digging around some more only to pull out my cell phone this time. "I—there were only three things in this pocket." Digging my hand once more into the seemingly endless depths of my pocket, I finally pull out the keys, only to drop my phone and lighter while trying to insert the key into the lock.

"Sorry." I glance sheepishly at Lumberjack, while I stuff my phone and lighter back into my pocket. He must have the patience of a saint because he just nods politely, even though he's weighed down by my three giant duffel bags on his back. The three duffel bags that now held everything that I own since I sold everything else to avoid paying for storage while in Alaska.

The lock clicks and the door swings open easily. The dank, lightness of the air that greets me is an unwelcome assault that causes my nose to wrinkle in repulsion. But it doesn't seem like Lumberjack is affected at all considering he just walks in and drops my bags on the floor.

Despite the smell, the cabin seems...cozy. The front door opens up to a living room, complete with an overstuffed couch, recliner, and a fireplace. There's nothing on the walls except for shelves with little wolf figurines lining them.

"Cozy..." I mutter under my breath.

Taking a step forward, I toss the keys on to a little table right next to the front door before Lumberjack clears his throat. We had agreed on a price for his services when I met him at the little airport I bought the snowshoes from, but he could demand more from me now. It's not like carrying my bags for me was included in that price. He took them from me when he realized how much I would slow us down if I continued to drag them behind me like I had been doing.

"Oh, right." I hold up my phone. "I'll send you the payment right now." I turn on my phone only to realize...there's no service.

He raises a brow at me as if he knew this would happen, and I sigh. "Don't worry...I have cash." I dig around one of the bags he dumped on the floor until I find my wallet. Hastily pulling my gloves off, I count out the bills.

I only had two-hundred in cash with me...I had planned on being able to pay him with a money transfer, but I guess that was on me for not clarifying with him. Disappointment fills my chest as I hold the folded bills out to him. At least I still have fifty on me. I had hoped to save the cash for an emergency situation...but, I suppose this is one. He doesn't waste a second, quickly flipping through the cash before shoving into his pocket. A nod of his head and he's all but rushing out the front door closing it behind him without as much as a goodbye.

"Alrighty then..."

Shivering, I take a good look at the room around me, realizing that for the first time in my life, I'm truly...alone. I've never truly been on my own in life. When Simon left, I had Mom. And then when she died, I had my grandparents. Even looking into my life when I went to college... I was never really alone. I lived in the dorms, and then had a roommate after graduation.

This is the first time in my life I'm completely, truly, 100% on my own.

Reality hits me in the face so hard I might stagger back. I'm an orphan. Sure, Simon hasn't been in my life, but he was alive, out there somewhere. Now he's not. So now, not only am I physically alone, here, in this cabin with nobody to hear me scream, but I also have no family, no friends...no anything.

The cold brushes my skin, thankfully shocking me out of whatever downward spiral I had entered. Not surviving the night would surely put a damper on whatever plans I had for this place. If there is one thing I learned on my hike up here it's that I may not have been made for this place, but I had to adapt, and quickly.

I need to get warm.

Moving towards the stone brick fireplace, I take note of the large stack of wooden logs in the corner. Simon had at least started preparing for winter before he met death. I may not know how to do a lot of the things he probably did, but...but I could start a fire. Right? I mean, I did watch like almost fifty videos on the way up on survival and life in Alaska. It can't be much harder than that.

Twenty minutes and seventeen curse words later, the fire is finally going. Removing my gloves, I let the heat seep into my frosty hands, willing it to penetrate the icy layer of cold on my skin. Once I'm sufficiently warm, I take a look around the rest of the cabin, the quiet, eerily reminding me of how alone I am.

It's like an entirely different world out here. Despite being somewhat peaceful.

As I look around, I try to piece together the kind of life my father lived, and what was so great about it that he would rather be here than with his own family. With his own daughter, especially after my mother died. I shake my head, washing out the memories.

Forget burning the place, I'll sell it. I'll have enough to write the book I've always wanted to and to live comfortably for a few years.

Yeah, that's a good plan.

Sell, write, live. Preparing my mental checklist, I pull out my laptop with the intention of checking the approximate value of the cabin online. Until, I try to turn on my hotspot and suddenly remember there isn't any service out here. Hell, no TV, either.

What the hell am I supposed to do to pass the time? Stare at the wall? I shiver at the memory of a short story I read in college about a woman who goes crazy because she is cooped up in her room and can't stop staring at the wallpaper.

Not a good idea.

Back home, if I wasn't on the hunt for a job, I spent most of my time watching TV or reading. I've always loved to read, so much so that I would put off other, objectively more important things for the sake of 'one more chapter'. Much to my chagrin, I'd had to leave my books with my neighbor…ex-neighbor, who looked at me like I was a crazy person when I begged them to watch my books for me while I was gone.

I can't imagine having made the trek up here with the addition of my giant book collection. The thought of it almost makes me laugh. I'd have really made a fool of myself then. So, as a result of some out-of-character logical thinking, I have nothing to read.

Hopefully, my old neighbor doesn't realize the value of my collection and sells them before I get back. I have some first editions in there that are worth a shit ton of money.

Scanning the room, my eyes fall on a bookshelf tucked into the corner of the living room. Speaking of books…they say nothing tells more about a person than the books they read, right? Unfortunately, perusing the bookshelf in the living room takes all of five minutes of my time to realize Simon was a very boring person. Ignoring all the books that aren't dictionaries or encyclopedias, I find four books.

A couple of medical journals, and a book on…wolf anatomy?

Wolf anatomy? What the fuck would he read that for?

I suppose maybe it's better that Simon wasn't in my life. Especially if he was so boring that *this* was his reading selection.

Seeing no other entertaining option, I opt to unpack the bags I brought. The bed sighs under the weight of the three huge duffels and I marvel that Lumberjack was able to carry them all the way here. Or maybe it's not that impressive and I'm just really out of shape.

Throwing my clothes in the armoire, I rifle through my other duffel. My alarm clock, my phone charger...my notebook, and a pen. A smile breaks out on my face. If I can't do anything else, perhaps I'll just get the book written now. I could have just used my laptop, but I cheaped out on the word processor software, which I can only access online.

However, with this journal and pen...maybe this journey to the middle of nowhere Alaskan wilderness can be a good thing after all.

I mean, there are tons of famous writers who go on trips in the wild to get away from things and write. Why can't I make this trip the same? Clear my mind, get my ideas down on paper. Who knows...maybe it can turn out to be the next New York best seller.

Before I can act more on the idea, an unexpected yawn makes me check the time. It's well past dinner and I haven't eaten anything in...and I don't recall when I ate last. Maybe on the plane? I shudder at the memory of the jerky, stale crackers, and questionable cheese that I chased with a flat beer.

Time for something more substantial.

Rifling through the pantry, I'm stunned to find the selection...lacking. Shouldn't he have had more food? There's a whole selection of canned goods, but his fridge is practically empty. Potatoes that have started to grow sprouts, a couple of moldy onions. He must have pretty good access to town so it doesn't make sense that this is all that he has with him. If it was hard getting food, no reasonable person would have let their stores get this low.

Then again, it has been a few months since his passing. Which makes sense.

The once silent cabin is soon filled with clanging and banging of me rifling through the pantry, desperate to find something I can just dump into a pot and heat up. My love of cooking is deeply outweighed by my desire to climb into bed and pass out.

That is until a red label catches my eye filling me with hope. Pulling it out from the deep recesses of the pantry, the can might as well be a trophy for how accomplished I feel.

"Ravioli it is."

By the time dinner is done and I've cleaned up, I'm beyond ready for bed. The sound of the wind picking up outside doesn't even bother me. All I want is sleep. I peek out the kitchen window and cringe. I might not know much about Alaska, but I know a blizzard when I see one. You can hardly see anything beyond the flurry of white on the other side of the glass.

But I refuse to let myself be disheartened. Food is a necessity, and while I was lucky to find the Ravioli...I should have been better prepared. It was stupid of me to think that after a few months of this place sitting empty that there would be sufficient supplies. So as soon as this blizzard is done, I have to get more food.

Otherwise I'm going to have real problems.

For now, I have to rest. I'm grateful for what I have and that the cabin is still warm. I don't even have to wear a jacket, which is a blessing considering my pajamas are practically calling my name and seeing the blizzard from my bedroom window seems to have the same effect on me that a rainy day does—makes me want to curl up under the covers with a good book.

Deciding that a book on wolf anatomy is better than nothing, I quickly change into my coziest pajamas and start to navigate towards the sparse bookshelf when I freeze.

There's no obvious explanation, but the hairs on the back of my neck stand up...it feels like I'm being watched. Like a deer frozen in headlights, I stare out the window, but can see nothing beyond the sheet of white.

An ear piercing howl slices through any sense of confidence I had accumulated in the last thirty minutes. *That sounded close.* Too close. Drawing the curtains closed as quickly as I can, I close the door to the small bedroom. My heart races as a million different questions roll through my mind.

The wolves can't actually get in here...right?

I shake my head. No, of course not. They would need thumbs to open the doorknobs, and wolves don't have thumbs. Plus I'm pretty sure I locked the front door. Unless there's some species of extra large Alaskan wolf that has thumbs and...and...and I'm an idiot. The wolves wouldn't need fucking thumbs, they would just need to knock down the door.

But why would they? I'm scrawny. All skin and bones as Grandma used to say.

Taking a deep breath, I step away from the door. I'm not even an appetizer to them. I barely scratch 5'2", a meager one-hundred and twenty pounds. There's plenty of deer, and...other animals that I don't know the names of that they would have to work less hard to eat. But then again, they wouldn't know that until they actually got in here, and then they might as well eat me for all the trouble they went through.

I'm fine. I'm fine. I'm *fine*.

Another howl pierces the air and I find myself scrambling to push the small wooden dresser in front of the door. And the bedside table. I'd have pushed the Armoire, but unfortunately, I wasn't blessed with the muscle ton to master the solid wooden structure.

Stepping back, I admire my handiwork. There's no harm in taking extra precautions. It's not going to hurt me to keep the door barricaded all night. Raiding the armoire drawers, I hope that my father was a cold sleeper just like I am and has extra blankets because the warmth of the fire definitely does not extend properly to this room.

Bingo.

The three throw blankets I found in the armoire envelop me as I huddle on the bed, closing my eyes tight. I try to calm the panic that has set within my mind causing my heart to race uncontrollably.

It doesn't matter if there are wolves outside. It's Alaska, so that's normal. Or at least that's what I tell myself as I jump at every sound and softly cry praying for daylight to come quickly so that I don't have to live the nightmare I'm currently in.

But nothing's working. It doesn't matter how much I cry and

fight against the urge to pick up my phone to call for help—knowing that there isn't any service—I can't.

I'm stuck here...in the middle of Alaska. Listening to the hunger of the wolves outside.

What the fuck have I got myself into?

Chapter 2

If My Life Was a Romance Novel

Lucy

Unbarricading the door the next morning is a lot more difficult when I don't have the adrenaline rush fueled by the fear of imminent death by my new imaginary breed of Alaskan Wolves—thumbs and all. It's only after I've broken into a sweat from my second round of furniture rearranging in the last 24 hours that I realize that the howling wind has stopped, even if it is still snowing.

So far, so good.

"First things first, I need coffee."

Pulling on the fuzziest pair of socks I can find, I mentally congratulate myself for having the foresight to pack for warmth during an Alaskan winter. My muffled footsteps are the only sound within the house as I make my way to the kitchen and rifle through the cupboards for a coffee maker.

The problem is searching high and low...I find everything *but* the damn coffee maker.

Though my little adventure of searching for it did allow myself to create a mental checklist of everything I need to survive my new life out here as an off-the-grid Alaskan writer.

"I need coffee, a place to write, my notebook, my pen...aha!"

Score...fucking coffee maker. I knew it.

I find the coffee maker in a cabinet above the fridge. The chair that I've brought over to reach that high squeaks as I climb off it with the prized machine in hands. "Now I just need to find coffee grounds and filter..." I mutter to myself as my eyes scan the room for where they could be located.

The filters ended up on the same shelf that the ravioli was on the night before. Next to them are two unmarked metal tins...I take my chances with the one on the left, prying the plastic lid open only to find dried oats.

I guess I know what's for breakfast. I hold my breath as I open the second tin before letting out another gasp. "Thank goodness, coffee grounds."

It's good that I can somewhat stand to drink my coffee black since there is no cream to be found, only sugar. But I can promise that is the first thing I'm putting in that fridge when I finally make it to town. I desperately need Caramel Macchiato-flavored creamer.

If they have it here, which by the looks of the town, I'll be lucky to get the basic shit.

Wandering into the living room and ready to start my day, I attempt to find a calming moment with myself, a clear path for how I want to begin this entire future in the wilderness.

All good writers find inspiration in nature, right?

If my life were a romance novel, this would be the point where I would slowly walk to the front door, my coffee in my hand and a blanket wrapped around my shoulders, and lean against the door frame as I contemplate my life. But instead, as I walk towards the front door, sans blanket, but with my cup of coffee, I remind myself that this is not a romance novel, and I certainly don't—

"Holy fuck," I breathe, staring at the statistical improbability in front of me. "There is a naked man...on *my* front porch."

Passed out on my front porch, more specifically.

And not just *any* old naked man, but a fucking *work of art*.

I could only see the backside of him but it's quite clear he is enormous. Not a mountain man, like my Lumberjack guide, but a man the size of a mountain. He must have gotten here after the blizzard calmed down because there's no snow on top of him. I pick my jaw up off the floor and set my coffee down on a small table next to the front door. This man must be freezing. He could die if I don't help him.

But what is he doing out here? And why is he *naked*? Maybe he's actually some Alaskan wilderness pervert who heard a lone girl moved into the cabin—

No. No, I can't think like that. What was it Mom used to say? "The best way to find out if you can trust somebody is to trust them." Mom was a sucker for Ernest Hemingway, and unfortunately, had passed that trait down to me.

My heart pangs. I can't believe it's been ten years since my mom died, and I still get choked up when I think of her. Mom would help him. A heavy sigh escapes me as I make the decision to do as Mom would do. After all, if I don't trust him, and he's innocent...he could die out here.

I reach for him, but quickly withdraw. He's naked. I mean, I knew he was naked and it was awkward enough to look at him, but now that I have to think about touching the naked man...my face heats up. It's been a while since I've seen a naked man, let alone touched one. But it's not like that. I am saving his life.

Right. How do I go about this?

He's face down, so I don't have any danger in encountering *that* area, but still. Dragging him by his arms might be a good idea. I reach for him, but shudder at the sudden image in my mind of his poor male parts, squished underneath him, dragging across the floor. I don't know the guy, but I couldn't possibly do that to him. Let me think...I could flip him over, but that still leaves the awkwardness of his front being exposed. What if he wakes up in the middle of me dragging him and thinks *I'm* the pervert?

Struck with an idea, I dash inside to my room, grabbing one

of the throw blankets and holding it up in front of me. It should be big enough, but barely. Rushing back to the front door, I lay the blanket out next to the man. Positioning it just right, I move around to his other side, ready to roll him onto the blanket that's already getting wet from the snow underneath it. Taking a deep breath, I get on my knees and brace myself to roll him over. As soon as my hands make contact with his skin, they withdraw in shock. This man should be freezing, or at least colder than me. But his skin is almost hot.

Huh. Because that's not weird.

He must be getting a fever from being out here in the cold. More resolved than ever, I steel myself yet again, pushing against the man's side. A good deal of grunting and two wet knees later, I've managed to roll him onto his back onto the blanket. Whew. Okay, now to reach around and put the other side of the blanket over him, to give him some semblance of privacy. I stand up, brushing off my wet pants of any lingering snow. Fisting the tail of the blanket, I lean back and pull with all my might.

He doesn't budge.

Come on, it's not like I'm *that* weak. Taking a second to breathe, I reevaluate my situation. He's on top of the blanket, which is good. That should make it easier to pull him because of....friction. Or something. Despite the fact that there's a blanket covering him, I can tell that he's well built. Dense muscle. Muscle means he'll be heavier, right?

Maybe if I lower my center of gravity...fuck, I only ever got a C in physics. Okay, but I should be able to do *this*. Crouching down, I squat as low to the ground as I can, fisting the blanket in my hand yet again and I *pull*. He ever so slowly, budges. My heart leaps. He budged!

Okay, Lucy, calm the fuck down and keep going.

As I pull him, little by little, the giant naked man slides further and further into my cabin. After what seems like hours, I've finally gotten him by the fireplace. My heart sinks when the realization of the fire being out confronts me. I suppose someone living up in this place should know what you're supposed to do, but that someone isn't me.

Huffing, I trudge over to the wood pile near the kitchen and grab a few logs. On top of everything else going on at the moment, the pile's eventually going to get low, which means I'm going to have to figure out how to get more soon. Maybe someone in town has some... or maybe this guy will know where I can get some when he wakes up.

If he wakes up.

Shaking my head, I ignite the fireplace once more with my lighter, and push the logs around with the poker until the fire picks up. *Phew.* I hadn't realized how frozen my hands, nose, and ears were until they were caressed by a wave of warmth, the delicious heat seeping into my skin.

I must look like a crazy person, my hair a tangled mess from sleeping in a pile of blankets, my sweatpants wet from the knees down. I should get changed so that Naked Guy doesn't think he's been kidnapped by some lunatic.

Leaving him safe by the fire, I head to my room to change. I can't say why I'm inclined to make a good first impression on a passed out naked man who obviously makes some very questionable life choices, but here we are.

Rummaging through the armoire, I search for something warmer, pulling out a pair of fur lined leggings, some more fuzzy socks, and a long sweater. It isn't the height of fashion, but in a place like this—fashion isn't important.

My long brown hair—littered with tangles—makes me wince as I run my brush through it trying to ensure I don't look like a crazed kidnapper. Though, I'm not sure why it matters. The guy literally showed up on *my* front porch. It wasn't like I sought him out.

Yet, regardless of how he got here I can't help but want to make sure I look as normal as possible. Or well—more presentable. I mean, I did save his life.

Maybe he'll thank me by buying me groceries.

Returning to the living room, I pick up my cup of coffee, hoping for it to heat me up from the inside. The sip that meets my tongue makes me recoil. Iced coffee is one thing, but coffee that was supposed to be hot and is now lukewarm at best...ew. Ignoring my stomach's demand for sustenance, I set my coffee back on the small table, content to ignore the growling sound coming from it for the time being.

Today is setting up to be wonderful.

Instead of making another cup of coffee, I opt to grab my journal and notebook, tucking my legs under me as I settle into the overstuffed chair closest to the fire. I know I should probably keep an eye on Naked Guy, but that doesn't mean that I can't write while I do.

Positioning my pen above the notebook, I don't know where to start. I know the idea in my head...my eyes are drawn towards Naked Guy. I didn't get a good look at his face earlier, what with my internal panic and trying to save his life and all.

The firelight plays across his face like a sunrise on glorious land. This man is gorgeous. A strong, broad nose, and a jawline so sharp it could probably cut glass. His brow is strong, over deep set eyes. And lips...I blush. It's dangerous to think about his lips. He has hair so dark, it's almost black, and it's mussed, barely grazing his eyebrows. I can't help but picture the color of his eyes once they open.

Would they be as dark as his hair?

Or perhaps a light blue, vibrant enough to rival the sky on a clear morning.

The last guy I dated, well, slept with, was a scrawny blond professor after I graduated. Not a professor from my school, I had consoled myself at the time, so it wasn't *that* bad. But the sex... that was definitely bad. Man couldn't find his way around a woman's vagina if I gave him a map...and a compass.

Despite this, he still felt the need to text me every now and again as if I would willingly subject myself to another two minute missionary humping session and him asking me if I came. Took every ounce of self control I had to not inform him that if he had to ask his partner if they came...they didn't.

But this man in front of me...the exact opposite of Horny Professor. And not just looks wise. I would bet my best set of high heels and a signed copy of my favorite book that this man could not only find his way around a vagina, but he knew exactly where he wanted to go and how to get there.

Not that I wanted him to get there. With me. No, I just met the guy. I'm saving him. But is it so wrong to want to know what color eyes the man I saved has?

I'm gazing at him so intently, so lost in my imagination of what could be waiting for me when his eyes open, that I don't even notice that his eyes *are* open, and he's been staring right back at me the entire time.

His eyes are blue. Shit.

Chapter 3

Shit Dads

Elijah

I've never thought of myself as a religious man, but if this is heaven, I'll convert in a heartbeat. The fuzziness of my memory isn't even a blip on my radar when staring at the woman in front of me, despite the fact I have no idea where I am or how I got here. Intense green eyes stare in my direction but not exactly at me, and she's slightly biting the bottom half of her sexy as hell full, pouty lips.

My wolf, in the back of my mind, whimpers at the sight of her.

Calm down, you bastard. She's a human. She can't be our mate.

Sitting in an armchair, her petite legs tucked underneath her, there's something about the way she's looking at me...shit, I think she must be lost in thought because she hasn't said anything since I opened my eyes.

Making a mental note of the state of my undress, I try to think back to how I got here. Last thing I remember is leaving with my pack to go hunting and then...nothing.

"Oh, fuck, you're awake." The woman's voice is like music, lilting and sultry.

"Barely," I grimace, my bones protesting as I sit up, keeping the blanket wrapped around me in an attempt to be somewhat of a gentleman. "Where am I, exactly?"

"Oh, um...my cabin?" Her cheeks flush, and she tucks a golden brown piece of hair behind her ear. "I'm sorry I'm not sure exactly where...I'm not from around here."

"No?" My eyes dart around the cabin, and I notice a distinct lack of...female touch. If I had to guess I'd say a man lived here. An unexplained sense of jealousy turns in my gut.

"I only got here yesterday," she admits, fidgeting with a pen in her hand, "and this morning, I was trying to see if the blizzard had done any damage, and I found you..." with each following word she turns a deeper shade of red, "on my front porch...naked." She's obviously uncomfortable about the whole nudity situation, but damn if her blushing isn't the most adorable thing I've ever seen.

A thought occurs to me. "How did I get in here from the front porch? I'm not a small guy, and you...no offense, but you're pretty small."

The flush leaves her cheeks, replaced by a fiery spark in her eyes. "I can be resourceful when I need to be." She gestures at the blanket wrapped around me. "I rolled you onto the blanket and dragged you in."

Her resourcefulness is impressive, I'll give her that. But her judgment? Dragging a passed out naked guy is not one of the best decisions someone can make. She's lucky I'm me and not a rogue.

"Well, thank you for taking a chance on me." I smile, even though I would have been fine if she had left me out there. Wolf shifters are hot blooded so it's exceptionally hard for us to get cold. Standing, I keep the blanket wrapped tight around me. I may be okay with nudity, but even I know that it's considered rude to show your naked body to someone you just met, much less a human, and for some reason, I care what this one thinks of me.

"Um...let me see something really quick." She gets up quickly and starts to walk toward another room. "I might have some clothes you can wear," she says over her shoulder.

"Oh, your boyfriend's clothes?" I call after her, unable to stop myself from staring at her ass as she walks away.

She doesn't answer me for a moment. Fuck. I probably just made a complete dick of myself.

"No," she finally calls back, coming back into the room with what looks like a tshirt and some basketball shorts, "this was my dad's cabin."

Relief floods my chest, but I shake it off.

What the fuck am I so relieved about? I don't even know this girl, and I'm looking for my mate.

"Was?" I find myself asking as I turn around, pulling the basketball shorts on. They're a little short on me, but they'll work. Turning back towards the girl, I toss the blanket onto a nearby couch. The way her eyes rove my body is not lost on me as I pull the shirt on. Again, a little small, but it's not going to rip or anything.

"He died," she says, not sounding nearly as sad as I would expect her to.

Hm. There was a human doctor studying wolves that lived near my territory who died recently...I wonder if it's the same man. I do feel like he mentioned having a daughter at some point.

"I'm sorry," I reply, not able to stop the sentiment from leaving me, even though she doesn't really seem all that broken up about it.

Tucking a stray piece of hair behind her ear, she gives a small smile. "It's fine...I didn't really even know him....he left my mom and I when I was seven. He just left the cabin and all his belongings to me."

"Still...it can't be easy." My voice is gentle, and I notice my arm reaching out for her before I stop myself.

What the fuck is that? It's like my arm just moved on its own.

She eyes me, not necessarily defensively, but warily enough that I feel stupid for not having control of my own damn limbs.

My wolf whines again.

"My dad..." I don't know why I'm volunteering one of my most painful memories, but for some unknown reason, I want her to know that I understand, to some extent. "My dad died a couple of years ago. He was a shit dad. Always too hard on us. Always cared more about the family business than his own kids." I find myself shrugging, "It wasn't until after he died that I realized I had so many things I never got to say to him. And that was what I was most upset about."

Her face is pensieve for a moment. "What did you want to say to him?" she asks softly, too softly, like she knows just how upset I was at the time.

Shrugging, I answer honestly. "That he was a shit dad, mostly."

Silence. Her hand is over her mouth, her eyes wide.

"Wha—"

Laughter bursts out of her. A laugh she obviously had been trying to keep in. "I'm so sorry." She giggles. "It's just that..." she continues wiping a tear from her eye, "that's what I want to tell my dad too. That, and 'what kind of dad leaves their daughter to come live in the middle of fuck-all Alaska'."

Raising a brow, I can't help from making a smartass comment. "I think we established that the answer to that question is 'a shit dad'." She rolls her eyes but smiles at me, and I continue, "but, as happy as I am to have company, I'm still sorry you're a part of the 'my-shit-dad-died-on-me-before-I-could-confront-him-with-my-feelings' club."

She grins at me. "A club that no ones happy they're a part of, but at least the members understand each other." I swear my heart skips a beat.

Suddenly realizing that it's a crime that I don't know this girl's name, I introduce myself. "I'm sorry, I didn't even introduce myself. I'm Elijah."

"I'm Lucy." *Lucy.* Her smile is damn near dazzling, and did my wolf just fucking *purr*?

"Lucy," I repeat, her name like a song in my ears.

"You must be starving," she says abruptly, turning around and walking away. "Let me make you something to eat."

"You don't have to do that..." I reply, only to have her toss a look over her shoulder that tells me I don't have a choice in the matter. Following after her, I take a seat at the small table in the kitchen while she busies herself, pulling out a metal tin out of the pantry.

"I hope you like oatmeal," she says sheepishly, "even if you don't, it's the only viable food in this fucking cabin."

Chuckling, I can't help but stare as I answer her, "oatmeal is perfect."

Though it does make me wonder why she would come up here without doing her research and preparing better. Last night's blizzard was only the beginning of what's to come and if she isn't prepared...she won't make it out here.

"So...Elijah," she speaks to me from over her shoulder, "what were you doing out in the woods during a blizzard? And *naked*? Like, did you start out that way or did you lose your clothes somewhere?"

"Did I start out naked?" I ask incredulously, holding in a laugh. She shrugs in response as if her question is more than reasonable given the current situation, which from an outsider's point of view, I guess it is.

Sighing, I think back to how I ended up here, the details coming back to me slowly. Fuck. I was with Riftan, my beta, and a couple of warriors when there was a rogue attack...I must have ended up on her front porch after the battle. I'm sure Riftan and the warriors are fine, the pack would have mindlinked me by now if they didn't return.

Okay. Selective truths. For some reason, I don't want to outright lie to her, but at the same time... "I remember I was out on a hunting trip with my friends—"

Not entirely a lie...

"Ah, that explains the nakedness." She turns her head just enough that I can see a raised eyebrow.

"Ha." I answer, rolling my eyes. "To be honest, that's the last thing I remember." She looks like she's about to say something, so I cut her off, "and no, I don't have a habit of getting naked while on hunting trips with friends."

She seems content with that answer, stirring the oatmeal, until she abruptly asks, "are they not worried about you?"

Strange. When was the last time anyone worried about me?

"They know I can handle myself," I explain, not knowing how to tell her that nobody would worry about me because I'm the strongest in the pack—next in line to be Alpha. "What about you?" Turning the question around on her, I prop my chin on my fist. "Is anyone worried about you, out here all by yourself?"

Her sigh is sad, so much that I might have taken the question back if I didn't want to know the answer so badly.

"No, my mom died when I was young, so I was raised by my grandparents who passed a couple of years ago while I was studying at Brown. My dad...Simon, was my last living relative, and he went and died on me too." Her pouty lips turned to a sad smile, spooning the oatmeal into two bowls. "So here we are. A city girl with no knowledge of anything wilderness or outdoors related, and a guy, who went on a hunting trip with his friends and ended up naked on said girls' front porch."

"Do you want to know what I think?" I don't know what it is about this girl, but I just cannot stop myself from trying to make her feel better.

She meets my stare, her breaths becoming more shallow. She swallows tightly before asking, "what do you think?"

"I think," without my consent, my body stands, and I take a step towards her, "that fact makes your situation all the more impressive."

She scoffs at me, her eyes never leaving mine. "Impressive? I—"

"A city girl," I take another step, "who knows nothing about the outdoors, braving the wilderness, and saving a passed out man on her doorstep? That sounds like a damn impressive person to me."

Her cheeks flush a deep shade of red, and I find that I might just have a new favorite color.

"Thank you," she says quietly, and so quickly I might not have caught it if I was human. Her eyes widen before she turns around, placing the bowls on the counter and leaving me standing in the middle of the kitchen.

Shit. Why does my body keep gravitating towards her? She probably thinks I'm some weird perv now. Quickly, I go sit back down in my seat at the table while she searches the cabinets.

"There you are," she announces, turning to me and grinning with a bag of brown sugar in her hand. "Do you want any?" she asks, spooning two heaping spoonfuls into hers.

"About half of what you put in yours." I grin, trying and failing to not seem over-friendly. "Do you have any milk?"

"Unfortunately, I was supremely underprepared when I got here, and have no idea where to get any sort of produce or dairy." She stirs both bowls, the steam curling up around her hand. "Then, I wasn't expecting the blizzard...are those common?"

A chuckle escapes me before I catch myself. "I wouldn't call that a blizzard." Clearing my throat, I catch the way her brows furrow at my words. "Blizzards are more...catastrophic. This is just a snowstorm. They're pretty common this time of year." My eyes are transfixed on her, even as she simply carries the bowls to the table. "It's standard practice to stockpile food."

She shakes her head as she finally reaches the table. "Still think my situation is impressive?"

My answer is instant. "Yes." I can't help but feel relieved that she doesn't seem put off or afraid of me, despite my body acting against my wishes.

Our eyes meet as she hands me the bowl. My fingers brush hers as I take it from her, and the spark is so intense, I nearly drop the bowl from shock.

My wolf howls. Could it be…?

"Elijah? Did you hear me?" Lucy is speaking to me as if she has been trying to get my attention.

I shake my head, my wolf won't stop howling.

Shut up, asshole!

"I'm sorry, what did you say? I zoned out for a second there." I try to play it off nonchalantly, but my mind is racing.

Her brow furrows in concern. "I said, you're welcome to stay here until the storm passes."

Stay here. I could do that.

She still has that concerned look on her face. "Are you okay? You did feel like you had a fever earlier…" She reaches across the table to touch my forehead, and there's that spark again. That fiery, blissful, *needy* spark. It's everything I can do to stop myself from throwing her on the table and claiming her, right here, right now.

She withdraws her hand, taking the sparks with her—both a blessing and a curse. "Huh. You don't feel that warm anymore." She shrugs, taking a bite of her oatmeal.

Numb to everything but one thought, I eat, but I don't taste anything. I stare at Lucy. It's impossible, she's human. And yet… and yet there's no denying the sparks that I felt not just once, but twice.

The instant attraction when I haven't looked at any female twice in years, the unfounded jealousy when I thought maybe another guy lived here…it all makes sense now.

Chapter 4

That's a Neat Party Trick

Lucy

"Coffee?" After finishing my oatmeal quickly, I'm looking for any way to break the tension that seems to have formed between Elijah and I in the last three minutes.

Elijah.

That's his name, and shit, if it didn't send a shiver down my spine when he had said mine. Something weird happened when my fingers brushed his. His eyes had widened, and he nearly dropped the bowl on the table. I felt a rush of excitement when he touched me, as brief as it was, but his reaction seemed more akin to static shock.

Even when my hand flew out against my will to check his temperature, his breath had stilled as trills of excitement shot up my arm. I can't explain it, and I'm not sure I want to.

This man, admittedly, was having an effect on me. I wasn't sure what it was about him that drew me in. Probably his beautiful face. Or damn near perfect physique. Or the way the sleeves of the t-shirt I gave him hugged his arms...

Fuck.

"Please." He nods, his eyes following me. His fingers lightly brush against mine as I hand him the mug. His shoulders tense slightly, his brow furrowing.

What is his problem?

I've never interacted with a man who seemed to have an issue with me touching him. Yet, everytime I touch him—there seems to be an issue. Did I do something wrong?

"Everything okay?" My voice is even as I observe him taking a sip from the mug.

He hesitates for a moment, his smile perking up once more as his gaze meets mine. "Yeah, everything's okay. Why?"

"No reason... just asking." I shrug. "Let me know if you need anything."

His response slightly grits on my nerves, though I'm not entirely sure why. It's like I know he's lying. Something's on his mind, and the fact that it could have been something I did and I don't even know what that is...bothers me.

Okay, fuck you too then, I guess.

Grabbing some coffee for myself, I set up my writing station for the day. My notebook and pen are on the table, I've got another cup of coffee. I should be ready. If I can only manage to concentrate and not let my mind wander to Elijah, whose eyes I can almost feel upon my skin.

Putting pen to paper, I try to write as the man across from me finishes his oatmeal. I'm determined not to stare at him, though the struggle is real. My eyes glare harder at the pen in my hand as I attempt to stay focused. The sight must amuse or something because a deep chuckle escapes from Elijah.

"Is something funny?" I ask, slightly more on edge than I should be.

He doesn't bristle at my tone, but rather takes it all in stride. "I'm just wondering what that pen did to you to deserve such a dirty look."

Ha.

"I'm just having a hard time getting started." I try to focus back on the page. Maybe it was the way that he tried to comfort me about my dad without even knowing me. Or the way that he told me I was impressive for having gotten this far with my current skill set.

Or the way I am acutely aware of the way his gaze is trained on me.

Sighing, I ignore the urge to check his expression. It doesn't matter what look is on his stupidly handsome face. Unless it's an expression that gives me an epiphany about this book I'm trying to write, it's useless.

My pen taps restlessly on the notebook, my bottom lip getting sucked under my teeth. This isn't getting me anywhere. And let's be honest, it probably isn't a good idea to get involved with a guy who showed up passed out and naked on my front porch anyway.

My eyes dart up, he's still watching me, a small smile on his lips as he slowly eats his food. Forcing myself to look away from his mouth and how his lips move around the spoon, I attempt to focus back on my journal. I can still feel his eyes on me, and only two sentences are written before I can't take it anymore. I'm just about throw my pen down and ask what the fuck he's staring at so hard, when his spoon clangs in his empty bowl, and he sets it down on the table.

Standing, he stretches, his shirt riding up to give me a glimpse of those perfectly sculpted abs again. "I really appreciate you letting me stay here until the storm passes." He nods towards his empty bowl. "And feeding me, of course. I'd love to repay your kindness somehow."

Shaking my head, I start, "you don't have to do—" but he isn't having any of it.

"I know I don't have to, but I want to." He gives me a lopsided grin before jerking a thumb over his shoulder. "I can do chores, dishes…make sure your generator is working properly."

"You—" Stopping, I shake my head. "Generator? There's a generator here?"

"Should be around the back," he says, "most cabins out here

have gas generators. We should probably make sure you have gas in the tank."

I nod numbly, what other essential survival facts am I completely unaware of?

"I noticed you were also running low on firewood," Elijah continues, "I can chop some for you."

I open my mouth to protest and stop. Why the hell am I keeping him from helping me? It's not like *I* know how to chop firewood. And besides, with him not in my immediate view, maybe I'll get some writing done. "Uh—thanks. I appreciate it."

"No problem."

He disappears out the back door and after a minute, he pops his head back in. "Your gas generator is about a third of the way full right now. Tomorrow I'll show you the way to town and we can get it filled up."

Tomorrow...wait, I'm going to be spending the night with him in here? I guess I didn't think about that when I offered for him to stay here until the storm passes. It'll be fine though, totally fine. I mean, I have a separate room... and there's a sofa and a chair out here.

It will totally be okay.

"Thanks." I smile, and he disappears outside once again. Watching after him, I realize how lucky I am that the guy who showed up on my doorstep isn't a serial killer.. I have no idea how long a third of a tank would have lasted me, but I would have been completely lost when the power went out.

Turning back towards my notebook, I take a deep breath and clear my mind with the full intention of getting some work done. Unfortunately for me, my seat at the table has a perfect view of the spot where Elijah is now chopping wood. And fuck does he look sexy doing it.

The soft sunlight is perfectly illuminating his features as he lifts his arms over his head, ax in his hands, before brutally swinging it down on the log of wood. His sharp, beautiful features are fixed into a look of pure determination. My mouth is dry. Realizing I'm staring, I quickly look back down at my notebook, clearing my throat.

This is going to be impossible. No matter how hard I try to stay focused on my poor empty notebook, I can't. My traitorous eyes find their way back to Elijah, and my mind slowly begins to wander. Not that I should let it. Getting involved with this guy is ridiculous. He isn't interested in me, he's just being nice.

But I can look, right? As long as I don't act on anything...

Looking is harmless. Looking is expected when a guy looks like that. God, his arms as they lift over his head yet again...I can see every dip and curve of his thick, defined biceps. The shirt stretches tight over his pecs, capturing every movement he makes.

Fuck me.

Now, wiping the sweat from his brow, he's taking off the shirt I gave him. How anyone can bear to be dressed in anything less than a fur coat out in that weather is beyond me, but who am I to complain about the view? His body glistens with beads of moisture that have somehow accumulated despite the near freezing temperature. He must run *really* hot.

As he wipes his face and body off with the t-shirt, my eyes follow the path the shirt takes. From his face, to the front of his body...his arms...my eyes catch on a tattoo on his collarbone that I hadn't noticed before. A crescent moon, black and white shaded, with a drop of blood hanging on the bottom point of the crescent. I lick my lips. I've always had a soft spot for guys with tattoos.

The sight of his arms flexing yet again as he demolishes another log spreads warmth deep in my belly...when was the last time I had been with a man? It had to be the Horny Professor five months ago. Elijah looks like he would be so much better than... whatever his name was. Like he would know exactly how to make a woman feel satiated. None of this one position, fuck until only he cums bullshit. My thighs clench together as I can't help but envision the way his arms would flex as he holds himself over me, or if he lifted me against a wall...

Lost in my thoughts, I jump at the sound of the back door slamming open. Elijah is standing in the door, his eyes dark and his gaze hard. I might be having an aneurysm because instead of the icy blue they once were, his eyes are almost completely black.

Did he...did he see me watching him?

My cheeks flush as I turn back towards my notebook. Quickly leaving the table, I pretend like I have something else to do and him re-entering the house is of no consequence to me. I can't believe I let myself get carried away like that. Sure, it's been a long time since I've been with a man, but that doesn't excuse me *ogling* him like some sort of creep.

I can't just ignore him though. If he didn't see me watching him, he'd know something was up by the way I left as soon as he came in the door. Trying to sound nonchalant, I call over my shoulder, "that was quick, did you get a a lot—"

My voice is cut off at the sound of a fucking *growl*. Whirling around, I'm faced with Elijah right behind me, his eyes back to their normal blue, breathing hard. "Don't make me chase you." His voice is a warning, one that almost scares me shitless. But the meaning behind his words makes the heat in my belly grow stronger, move lower. I try to play dumb.

"I don't know what—"

"Don't play dumb," he says slowly, "don't pretend like you have no idea what I'm talking about."

"Maybe I am dumb." Refusing to meet his gaze, I keep my head down. "Maybe I'm as stupid as a bag of rocks. You don't know me."

"I know you more than you think," he replies, raising a brow.

Cocky bastard.

At my silence, he continues, "did you like what you saw, Lucy?" His voice is deep, sensual, as he takes another step toward me. My name on his lips sends another wave of heat through me. I back up, my back hitting the wall as he cages me in, one hand on either side of my head. I can't help but stare at the biceps that had me almost soaking my panties only moments before.

"Someone's rather full of themselves," I challenge, daring to meet his eyes, searching for any hint of the man who had consoled me about my father. Determined to keep my eyes off his bare chest, I can feel his breath on my cheek as he breathes hard, almost like he's physically restraining himself from being all over me.

It's hot as fuck.

"While that's not untrue," his expression slightly relaxes and he arches a brow, his nostrils flaring, "it doesn't change the fact that you're wet right now."

My cheeks heat yet again and I avert my gaze. "How would you possibly know?"

"Trust me. I can tell."

"That's a neat party trick," I deadpan, and his expression doesn't change. "Is this your plan? Pretend to be passed out naked so I bring you into your house so you can make a move on me?" I ask, sounding braver than I feel.

"Not at all." His voice is quiet. "You started this, Lucy. If you want me to move, tell me, and I will. Tell me to fuck off and leave your cabin, and I will." He swallows. "Tell me to kiss you...and I will. I am absolutely, completely...indecently, at your disposal."

Holy fucking shit.

His eyes are calmer now than when he burst into the kitchen...but there's something behind them I can't quite place. Yearning? Tenderness? A sort of...possessiveness? For some inexplicable reason, I know, deep down, that he wouldn't hurt me.

Yet, part of me wants him to...it the most delicious kind of way.

My heart is pounding so loudly I'm sure he can hear it. Do I want this? Obviously, I want him. But staring from a window and being faced with it in the flesh are two completely different things. Searching his eyes, his gaze has softened considerably and he's looking at me like...I don't even know what to make of the look he's giving me. But despite the fact that Elijah is a beast among men, I don't feel like prey. I feel...safe.

"Lucy..." he whispers, and I look at him. *I want this.*

"Kiss me," I breathe out.

Chapter 5
Well, Shit

Lucy

He kisses me like he's drowning and I'm a breath of fresh air. Like he's been starving and I'm a feast. The way that he kisses me… there's no fucking way I just met this guy. Because he kisses me like he's been waiting for me. And the chemistry…I mean, that has to be it. How else do I explain the feeling of pure euphoria that blooms and spreads every time he moves his lips against mine?

Our lips move together as if made for each other, and the moment that his tongue sweeps across my bottom lip, I stifle a moan, opening up further to grant him access. Our tongues dance together, and I bite his bottom lip, earning a growl from him. Before he pushes me further against the wall, he lifts me by the backs of my thighs so that my legs wrap around his waist.

Having him possess me is intoxicating. It's like every inch of my body's on fire as my hands tangle within the locks of his hair. The basketball shorts he's wearing do little to hide the evidence of his desire, and it's all I can do to not grind myself against him.

"Fuck, Lucy," he gasps between kisses, moving one hand from under my ass to palm my breast in his hand. I moan into his mouth as he massages it, my nails digging into his back. He weaves his fingers through the hair at the base of my neck, using it as leverage to tilt my head to the side as he kisses my mouth, before slowly letting his lips trail down my neck. Pausing at the spot where my neck connects to my shoulder, he licks and sucks, sending an unexpected bolt of pleasure through me.

Fuck, I was right. He does know what he's doing.

He shudders at the moan that escapes my lips, and he pulls back, staring at me, as both of our chests heave trying to catch a moment of clarity. "I want you, Lucy," he says, his voice husky, as his eyes trail over my face, as if trying to memorize every line and angle, "all of you."

Swallowing, I nod my head. Yes. I want this too. I don't know the last time I've ever wanted anything so badly in my life. His eyes almost look black as his mouth devours mine once again, still holding me as he walks us down the hall, down the hall towards my bedroom.

I'm downright giddy as he walks me into my room, before gently laying me on the bed, separating us from our kiss as his arms flex, holding himself over me. My stomach flips in anticipation.

Shit, they look even better than I had imagined.

His eyes rove my body as he looks at me, and even though I'm fully clothed, I may as well be completely bare before him. "You're so beautiful," he says so softly it's almost a whisper, before lowering his mouth to mine once again. Gone are the frantic, soul consuming kisses from the hallway.

The way he kisses me now is slow, like he's memorizing the feel of me, the taste of me. Like there's nothing else he would rather do than lay here with me. His kisses move away from my mouth once again, trailing lower down my neck. A little nibble has me giggling out, "talk about repaying my kindness."

His body stills. The kisses stop. Lifting his head to look me in the eyes, he speaks slowly, "please tell me that was a distasteful joke."

"Well, yeah, it's a joke." My brow furrows, confusion taking hold. Don't tell me he thought... "Obviously, I'm not doing this so you can repay me for feeding you shitty oatmeal, but..."

He stands, backing away from me. Suddenly cold without his body heat, I sit up wrapping my arms around me.

"But what?" he asks, his face unreadable.

"But..." Shrugging, I don't look at his face. "I mean, we just met. It's not like it actually means anything, right? It's just sex." I'm all for relationships, but can he really expect to get an actual commitment from me after knowing me for a few hours?

"What the fuck did you think I was talking about when you said I wanted all of you?"

I'm taken back by his comment. My mind, a complete whirlwind of confusion as I try to figure out what the hell is going on. One minute we're kissing and the next, he's acting like I just told him his puppy died or something.

"Hold on...what the hell is going on? Why are you pissed off at me?" I ask, my voice turning angry, "I just met you...I mean I'm all down to fuck, but now I'm unsure considering the way you're acting."

"I meant..." He hesitates, running a hand through his hair. "*All* of you. Not just your body."

*The audacity. What the hell has he done to deserve **all** of me?*

"I don't *do* one night stands. Never have." His hands run through his hair as he walks back and forth between my bed and the door. "If you sleep with me, you're mine forever." His pacing stops, and his eyes meet mine, determination lining his sky blue irises. As far as he's concerned, he is absolutely, 100% in the right about this.

He doesn't do one night stands? With the way he just kissed me, I call bullshit.

"Yours forever?" Scoffing, I repeat his words back to him, hoping he'll hear how crazy he sounds. "What century are you from, Elijah? I'm a person, not a fucking piece of property."

Annoyed, I stand, marching to the living room. Elijah's footsteps follow me. "I know you're not a piece of property. But I don't do just sex. That's not how I'm wired." He reaches for my hand, but this time the thrill that runs up my arm doesn't excite me, it pisses me off.

I whirl on him, ripping my hand out of his grasp. "And I'm not wired to sleep with possessive assholes, so we're both out of luck."

Hurt flashes across his face briefly. "I didn't mea—"

"I haven't worked my ass off my entire life, striving to make a life for myself just to end up belonging to some...guy!"

"I'm not just 'some guy', Lucy! And you're not just some girl, you're—" He stops, pursing his lips as if trying to decide what to say next. His mouth gapes open, but words don't escape.

"I'm what? What on earth could I possibly be to justify you trying to..." Searching for the right words, I throw my hands in the air in frustration, "trying to, to *own* me, less than twenty four hours after meeting me?"

His silence is infuriating.

"Whatever. It's done. Mood—officially killed." I stalk to the kitchen, his footsteps once again echo behind me. "Don't follow me," I bark over my shoulder.

"I'm not." His voice is clipped. "I need to cool off." We reach the kitchen and he continues past me, walking out the back door.

Well, shit.

That went...poorly. How did it start as the hottest makeout session of my life and turn into...this? It's not like I'm completely against the idea of possibly being something more to *someone* in the future, but now? That's coming on a bit strong.

I barely know the fucking man. I'm not crazy, am I?

Sighing, I sit back down at the table exactly how I was before Elijah had burst in here like a madman, somehow sensing how turned on I was. That had to be bullshit. He just saw me staring at him through the window, practically drooling. Doesn't take a genius to figure out what that means.

A pang of guilt hits my chest. He was right, I did start this. I started this when I couldn't stop staring at his ridiculously sexy body and the way he was chopping wood for me like he was a piece of fucking meat.

Then, I all but laughed in his face when he suggested this was more than just sex. And if my memory of my senior prom is correct, when Emmett Storven had me half dressed in his hotel room after the dance, I cried, running from the room when Emmett laughed at the notion of actually having feelings for me, asking what I expected besides sex.

And I just did the same fucking thing to him.

Fact is, we aren't teenagers. It's not the same thing. Besides, it's not like I couldn't have feelings...I enjoy his company, he makes me laugh, he's sweet and kind.

But I didn't tell him that. No, instead I called him a possessive asshole.

Fucking brilliant.

Maybe I can apologize when he comes back in. Maybe I can tell him that I do really like him, and I'm open to getting to know each other better before making any crazy commitments. In the meantime, we can either have sex like crazy but realize it isn't tied to type of committment...or, we can wait and see where things go.

I'm not sure how either of us will survive the second one if we are already trying to jump each other's bones after less than a day.

Yes, that's what I'll do. Give him time to cool off, and then when he comes back inside, we'll talk like mature adults. Nodding to myself, I pick up my pen and start writing. The last couple of days, it seems like writing has become my way of feeling in control. If I can't control what's going on in my life, at least I can control what I put on the page. I took one psychology course as part of my general education, but I feel like that's a fair analysis. Three words in, and I look out the window. I want to talk to him now. I can't stand the thought of him being upset.

I haven't had a long term relationship since the day that Tim Melrose broke up with me on the first day back to school our junior year of high school. Apparently, Bianca Lemmings had gotten an ass and great tits over the summer, and I...well, I didn't.

A late bloomer, Grandma used to call me. Apparently my mom didn't even get her period until her 17th birthday, her curves filling in much later. While I wasn't *that* far behind, I did grow a cup size over summer break a year later and suddenly little old Timmy realized what a 'mistake' he made. Luckily, I did not fall for him again.

I sigh as I remind myself yet again that I'm not in high school anymore, or even college. And Elijah sure as hell isn't Tim Melrose.

I'm open.

I'm flexible.

I'm a mature, responsible adult.

Standing from my spot at the table, I march to the back door, wrenching it open, completely unprepared for the cold that assaults me. Sharp chills kiss my cheeks as I lean my head out the door, scanning the area. Thank fuck for fur-lined leggings.

Shit, he went out in only basketball shorts in this *cold?*

I don't see him. He's not chopping wood, he's not anywhere in the trees. Shit...I hope he didn't try to walk home in his state of undress. I don't know how far it is, but surely he'll freeze to death, no matter how warm his body runs.

Something in my peripheral catches my eyes, and glancing to my side, I see a pile of firewood stacked right next to the door, against the wall. There's no way he did that before coming inside earlier. He must have done it just a moment ago. Smiling to myself, I shut the back door, leaving it unlocked for him. Maybe I didn't screw this whole thing up after all.

Before I know it, the sun has set, and he still hasn't returned. With dinner done, and me having already eaten, I contemplate what to do next. It's not like I can go out there searching for him...I'd end up dying in the snow. He actually lives here, I don't.

Frowning, I scrawl a note on a piece of paper from my journal, ripping it out of the book. 'Key under that rock' it says with an arrow pointing diagonally toward the biggest rock I was able to lift to place the key under. Taping the paper to the door, I step back, admiring my handiwork. I know I could probably just get away with leaving the key taped to the door or something, but with how heavy the key is and the chill in the wind...it probably would have fallen off before he ever saw it. At least the paper is lighter, and hopefully won't blow away.

My eyes scan the note...something is missing. Raising my pen to the paper, ignoring the awkward angle of writing on the door, I add underneath, 'Can we talk? I didn't mean what I said.'

Well, I meant some of the things I said. But not all of them.

There. Now, hopefully he comes back, and we can talk this out. If he decided to just leave, though...my heart pangs. I hope he comes back. I know I'll regret it if he doesn't.

Busying myself with dishes from the day, my thoughts are consumed by Elijah. On how having him around felt. To the way he kissed me, and then the angry words said between us. I barely know the man and I can't help but feel like I've known him forever.

I hope he's okay. I know he said that people don't worry about him, but doesn't everyone need someone to worry about them?

What if my note on the door was a bad idea? No, wolves can't read, so it will be fine. That's what I tell myself as I look out the window before going to bed, my eyes glued to the two wolves watching me from the treeline.

Chapter 6

Eh, I'm Not That Hungry Anyway

Lucy

My room is barely lit by the rising sun outside when my eyes crack open. Rolling over, I take a peek at the time on the clock next to the bed. 10:15 am.

Fuck, I can't believe I slept so late.

Despite being annoyed at the time, I snuggle deeper into the warmth of my mountain of blankets, closing my eyes and trying to keep myself from replaying the events of the day before in my head.

How is it that this man, who quite literally fell into my life only 24 hours prior, has such a chokehold on me? Shivering at the memory of the way he kissed me on this very bed, I resolve to be productive despite my disappointment.

Throwing the covers off of me, I make my way to the kitchen to get some coffee and breakfast going. I stop short at the sight of a note on the kitchen table. Picking it up, I realize that it's the same note I had put on the door, and there was writing on the other side,

'I want to talk to you too. I have some pack business to take care of, but I'll be back tomorrow. You looked too cozy to wake.

-Elijah'

Pack business? Maybe it's some Alaskan-specific job term. I don't even know what he does for a living. I'll have to ask him when he comes back. His note puts a pep in my step, knowing that I'll see him again and that I didn't completely ruin everything yesterday.

After coffee and breakfast, I'm ready to get some writing done. *Finally.* The story…the daughter of a duke meets a handsome stranger, only to find out he's from the very family who rivals hers…it's not the story I started off with, but the words come easily to me, my mind forming the sentences before I write them. Spending the better part of the day writing, crossing out bits, then writing again, I almost forget to eat lunch. I remember seeing some jerky on the top shelf of the pantry when I was searching for the coffee maker.

Tearing a bite off the jerky, I continue writing, ignoring the cramping in my hand. This is what I came out here to do. This was my goal, and warmth spreads throughout my chest as I realize I'm finally making headway.

Turning the notebook to a fresh page, my pen scratches the paper, and the warmth in my chest immediately dissipates, replaced by the cold force of reality, who, by the way, is a total bitch.

"No!" I practically screech, shaking the pen in the air. "No, no, this fucking pen! You're supposed to be lucky, damn you! Don't you dare run out of ink on me!" My voice, echoing in the empty cabin, does nothing to persuade the pen to magically fill with ink, and no matter how many times desperately I run it over the paper, I have to accept the fact that my only pen ran out of ink. Throwing the pen across the room in defeat, I bury my head into my folded arms on the table.

After all this time, trying so hard to get somewhere on this… this, the *one* fucking thing I wanted to do while I was out here. And a fucking pen is the one thing standing between me and actually getting something done. If I had just shelled the money out for the damn word processing software, none of this would be happening.

Actually, if my dad had never abandoned me, moving to the middle of the fucking Alaskan wilderness, then suddenly dying, leaving me everything he owns, amongst which is one cabin with *no fucking internet*, then this would never have happened.

So, reasonably, I deduce that this is actually my dad's fault. If he had never left, never would have ended up here. Tears prick my eyes, leaving me wishing I could tell him that myself.

Fuck him. I will not cry.

Lifting my head, ignoring the tears that are threatening to emerge, I scan the room. There's plenty of cupboards and drawer space. There has to be a fucking pen in here *somewhere*. In desperation, I tear through the kitchen, opening drawer after drawer, cupboard after cupboard. Behind the fridge, above the oven, it doesn't matter if no sane person would hide their pens in the crack between the stove and counter, I'm checking there too.

Once the kitchen is sufficiently torn apart, I move to the bedroom. Every nook and cranny, every drawer, even under the fucking mattress. It doesn't matter if logically, there's no way that there would be any pens hidden under the mattress. But I can't truly say that I've looked everywhere if I don't actually look, well, everywhere.

Suddenly I'm twelve again, scouring my grandparents house for the last thing my mom gave me before she died. A gold locket with her initials on it. She had pushed it into my hands and told me to always know that she was with me. She had tubes under her nose and an IV in her arm, but she seemed more concerned about me than anything. I had it on during the flight to New Hampshire to live with my grandparents, but the next morning, I couldn't find it. I was convinced that it was somewhere in the house. I tore every room apart, impossible to reason with even as my grandparents tried to tell me it might be gone. That maybe it somehow fell off on the plane.

It wasn't until I had torn apart their house, every nook and cranny, every shelf, corner, and drawer, leaving their home in complete chaos was it that I broke down and cried. I didn't leave my room for three days.

But I would not be defeated this time. There has to be a pen somewhere in this damn house, and I *am* going to find it. Moving to the living room, I check any drawers and shelves I can find. Checking behind the ridiculous little wolven figurines, I curse when I almost knock them over. Looking on the fireplace mantle is pointless, but I do it anyway. Removing all the couch cushions and checkin in the cracks is fruitless as well.

Sighing, I sit cross-legged on one of the couch cushions on the floor in front of the fire. Scanning the room for anything I might have missed, and that's when something catches my eye on the very top of the bookcase. Is that...a cup?

I can make out some shapes in the cup and it looks like it might be pens but there's no way to be certain. Unless...so eager to claim my prize, I don't waste any time getting a chair from the kitchen, I test one of the bottom shelves with my foot. This should hold me. Planting one foot on the next shelf, I reach my hand up as far as it will go, but I still come up short. I attempt another foot on the next shelf up but—

"Fuck!" Yelling, I fall back onto the floor, bringing the bookcase halfway down with me. Luckily for me, it's anchored to the wall. Though I'm not being crushed by a bookcase, I will be assaulted by the encyclopedias and rained down on by pens. I brace myself, throwing my arms up to deflect the impact of the books, but nothing comes.

Huh.

Slowly lowering my arms, I peek over them at the bookcase. The encyclopedias are...it looks like they're actually anchored to the bookshelf. My quest for a pen momentarily forgotten, I stand and push the bookcase so it's flush against the wall again. Brushing my hands off on my pants, I try to physically pry the books off the shelf, but they don't move. In fact, upon closer inspection, it looks like it's not a bunch of books at all, but a box, cleverly painted and carved to look like a set of encyclopedias at first glance. I have to admit, it's genius if you want a good hiding place for something. I mean, who the hell would willingly read an encyclopedia?

But what was he hiding?

My brows furrowing, I feel the sides of the box. Hm. There's no keyhole, no switch. I run my hands all around the box, even straining my hands to reach the back. Finally, my fingers find a divet in the back that feels like a button. Holding my breath, I push in, and hear a satisfying click as the top of the box rises slightly.

Lifting it the rest of the way, I peer into the box and find... notebooks?

Pulling one out and flipping through it, vaguely familiar penmanship glares at me. Was this...was this my dads writing? The word 'happy' jumps out at me from the page and I realize it's written the exact same way as every birthday card he's sent me, where he would scrawl, 'Happy birthday, Lucy. Love, Dad.'

Each page has a date at the top, the one I'm holding is from five years ago. Eyeing the rest of the books, I wonder how far back these journals go. If there's anything about why he left mom and me. About what he was doing out here.

Before I can think better of it, I remove the other four notebooks from their hiding places and move back to the cushion on the floor. In front of the fire, I lay out each notebook, the earliest on my left, the most recent on right, the three in the middle in chronological order.

Well, I was *looking for something to read.*

Picking up the earliest notebook, my body tenses, like I'm a kid sneaking into the cookie jar and I think mom or dad is coming.

After oh-so cheerfully reminding myself that both my parents are dead, so there is literally no one to catch me, I open the book, checking the date. Doing the math, I quickly calculate…eighteen years ago.

My heart quickens.

That was the year before he left us.

Reading, it's like I'm being transported into my father's mind. Though even in his own journal, he is somewhat cryptic, as if he's afraid of someone reading them. He mentions his work as a scientist, researching genetic mutations. He felt like he was often being watched and would often hear wolves howling.

Okay that's weird.

I read through the rest of the journal, which was mostly uneventful, except for the last few pages. It's not necessarily a diary; it's not full of feelings, but it's not all work related either. I read right up until he says a hulking man approached him at work one day, and then…it cuts off. It's like the remaining pages were torn out of the book.

Immediately picking up the next book, I look at the date. It's dated a few months after he left us. Defeated, I place it back on the floor. I don't understand. In the first journal, he seemed… happy. Not discontent with his life at all. He loved us. It's not like he writes on and on about his love for me and Mom, but, I can tell. In the subtle way he remarks on the sound of mom's laugh one time when I tried to talk with a mouth full of marshmallow. And the way he detailed the exact number of freckles on my nose.

What happened in between these two books that ended up with him leaving in the dead of the night with only a note to my mom saying, 'I'm sorry, I can't let it happen. I'm leaving.' I was still so little only five at the time, but I remember the gut wrenching sound of my mom sobbing into her friend's shoulder the next morning from behind a closed door, saying that she didn't understand the note.

"What does he mean, he can't let it happen? Was our marriage *doing* something to him?" She had choked out, completely blindsided. All her friend could do was murmur comforting words, which I couldn't make out.

Something is missing...it didn't add up. Checking the time, I grab the second book and take it to the kitchen with me, reading it with one hand while I search for something to eat for lunch.

I'm deep into the second notebook by the time I finish some instant noodles. Shit, I really need better food. But Elijah said he would take me to town to get food at some point, so I shouldn't worry. At least, I try not to worry. If he doesn't come back tomorrow like he said he would, I was going to have to figure something out.

Taking all the books into my room, I set up camp on the bed, reading through the journals until the moon is high in the sky and I'm sure I've missed dinner.

Eh, I'm not that hungry anyway.

The second book details the way to town for food, how he'd had a gas generator set up, and how he'd continued his research on genetic mutations since arriving in Alaska. I'd been laying on my side, a hand propping my head up, reading the book that was laid flat on the bed, when a phrase jumps out at me, causing me to sit upright, the book in my hands.

"The werewolves are restless. They've allowed me to live on the border of their lands, but I need to make progress if I want to keep my freedom"

The fuck? Werewolves?

New theory, my dad moved out here because he was going crazy.

A howl slices through the air, nearly making me jump out of my bed, and glancing out my window, I make out two pairs of red eyes staring at me from the treeline. And a shiver runs down my spin.

Fucking wolves.

Drawing the curtains closed, I settle back into bed, my eyes burning with exhaustion as I continue to read the journals. There's no way that werewolves exist, and even though the journals say a lot, they still have me confused as to why he left and what he was doing here.

I'm only vaguely aware of my eyes slowly drifting shut, when the sound of howls echo through my ears once more. Thoughts of werewolves, and my father, and mystery around this cabin plaguing me until I finally drift into darkness.

If there's something I'm missing, I'm going to find it.

Chapter 7

Something Like That

Lucy

Chopping firewood is fucking hard. Elijah had made it look so easy, but here I am, struggling like an idiot to cut a damn log in half. I was on my third cup of coffee this morning, needing the extra boost due to the absolute mess I had to clean up from the day before when I realized that the firewood was getting low again.

I mean, yeah, Elijah just cut some. But who the hell knew that it would go that quickly?

Trying not to be bothered that Elijah still hadn't shown his face yet, I hike the ax over my shoulder, just about to bring it down on the log, when a voice behind me calls out, "you're holding the ax too tight."

Holy fucking shit!

I jump slightly, my heart fluttering in my chest as I freeze in my place. Somehow, I've already become so accustomed to his voice that I knew it was him without even turning around. "Maybe I wouldn't be holding it too tight if I had someone to show me how to do this properly," I reply playfully.

Suddenly, I feel breath near my ear as a chest pushes against my back. I'm enveloped by his body as his hands cover mine, sending trills of excitement down my arms as he slightly loosens the death grip I have on the ax. "Like this," he murmurs softly, and I'm holding my breath as he helps me arc it downward onto the log, a small grin of triumph appears on my face as I look at the broken pieces on the floor.

Mourning the loss of his body heat as he steps back, I turn, dropping the ax on the floor. "You came back," I say, my voice breathless at the sight of him.

A look of guilt briefly crosses his face as he rubs the back of his neck. "I'm sorry. I was out cooling down, and then my pack contacted me...we've been having some security issues."

"Your pack? Is that some kind of new-age corporate leadership term?" I blurt out, watching a smile form on his face before a chuckle slips from between his lips.

"Something like that."

My gaze runs over him, taking in how different he looks now that he's dressed in his own clothes, and his hair is actually done. "Looks like you're wearing clothes that actually fit you," I tease, noting the way his navy blue half-zip sweater makes his eyes pop. He looks like he was made to live out here with his sweater, dark wash jeans, and brown leather lace up boots.

While on the other hand, I'm shivering in a beanie and my puffer coat, with no idea what it takes to survive this bullshit cold weather. It's honestly crazy how he can go around with so few layers.

The corner of his mouth tugs upward. "I had to trade in the basketball shorts, I'm afraid."

"What a shame." I can't seem to tear my eyes away from him, it's like he's a damn magnet. His gaze meets mine with equal intensity, the silence stretching between us. Clearing my throat, I look away for just a moment, just enough to break the spell. "Did you want to come in for dinner? I think I have a couple more cans of ravioli...maybe a few more instant noodles, but..."

His eyes light up, and without explanation, he jogs over to the treeline where he must have been watching as I struggled to chop wood. Reaching behind a tree, he pulls out three paper bags, all overflowing with food. "I come bearing gifts." He grins, walking toward the cabin.

He brought me food. I'm so fucking relieved to have something real to eat my eyes nearly start watering. Running after him, I open the kitchen door, and help him unpack all the groceries.

"I never got to take you to town for food," he explains, pulling a pack of wrapped up red meat out of the bag, "so it's the least I could do."

"The least?" My jaw drops in disbelief as I pull out a small container with brown eggs, followed by a loaf of bread, something that looks like pasta, and thank god, coffee creamer. Even if it is the cheap powdered kind. "I would have appreciated this even if it was just more canned goods, but you..." Shaking my head, I place a hand on his forearm. "Thank you, Elijah."

"Don't thank me yet," he grimaces, "I don't know how to cook any of this." He grabs a box of mac and cheese. "Maybe I could do this. But not much else. And you won't believe how lucky I was to even find this."

"Lucky for you." I snatch the box out of his hand and put it in the pantry. "I am an *amazing* cook...but what do you mean lucky to find it?"

"Well," he begins another gorgeous smile on his lips. "The town nearby doesn't have a wide variety of things to choose from. You usually have to get lucky with things. They only get shipments every so often and things like mac n' cheese and other normal foods you find on the mainland aren't often found here."

"Jesus, that must suck."

Again, he laughs. "Yeah. My family is fortunate enough that we have our own plane so we do shopping for stuff like that once a month and in the next largest city to where we are. They usually have more of a selection. But still nothing like where you came from."

I hadn't actually taken any of that into consideration when

moving her. My primary focus had just been getting here. Not how life would be once I got here. Or the difficulties I might find.

An hour and ten dirty dishes later, we're sitting in the kitchen, our plates full of what Elijah says is deer and spinach bread, which I was surprised about, as well as rice. "This looks amazing." Elijah nearly drools, cutting a piece of the deer and piling rice on top of it. Taking a bite, he nearly moans, "*Tastes* amazing."

Suppressing a grin, I take a sip of the white wine Elijah brought with him, "Told you."

"I never doubted you," he says, stuffing his face. "Where did you learn to cook like this?"

"My mom." Smiling at the memory of our days in the kitchen, I continue, "she was a professional chef at one of the most high end restaurants in town. I wanted to be just like her. So, after begging and begging, she finally relented, and every Tuesday night she would teach me a dish and then I would be the one to make us dinner. That went on for about two years...before..." Tears fight their way to the surface and I mentally scold myself.

Now is not *the time to start crying about your dead mom!*

Shaking my head, I continue, "I kept the tradition. Every Tuesday night I try a new recipe. But every other night, I practice the old ones too. Makes me feel like...she's not so far away."

"I'm sorry," Elijah reaches a hand across the table to grasp mine. "I didn't mean to—"

"No," interrupting him, I squeeze his hand, then move to pick up my fork. "I'm fine. What about you? What's your family like?"

Luckily, he doesn't seem offended at my change of subject. "As you know, my dad died a couple of years ago. That just leaves me, my mom, and my little sister."

"Are you close with them? Are they also a part of the family business? I still don't even know what the family business is, by the way." At least assaulting him with questions helps to drive the memories of my mom from my mind.

"My little sister, Bailey, is a bit of a busy body. My mom is heavily involved with the...family business. That is, until I can take over."

"Oh? What do you need to do to take over?" My curiosity piques, propping my chin on my fist.

"It's not so much something I need to do..." His words are slow, like he's choosing them carefully, "so much as it is something I need to find."

I may not know much about running a business or anything like that, but I've never heard of someone saying they have to 'find' something in order for them to take over their family business. Usually it's left to them when someone dies or like a transfer or something.

"What do you need to—"

"More wine?" he interrupts, rising abruptly from the table.

Okay, I guess we're done talking business.

Noticing the topic must be touchy for him, I can only sigh as my gaze follows him. "Sure."

He grabs our glasses, heading to the counter to refill them from the bottle he had brought while I begin to gather the dishes off the table. When he turns, he quickly stops me. "Let's worry about that later," he says, motioning towards the living room. "Let's sit by the fire."

There's something within the depths of his gaze that makes me hesitate before slowly nodding. There have been times since I first met him that he says something that makes it seem like he's almost from a different world. As if he knows things I couldn't begin to understand. I just haven't quite put my finger on what it is.

Settling on the couch by the fire, I tuck my feet under me, Elijah sitting on the opposite side, "So," I start, sipping from my glass, "why did you bring wine?"

"Do you not like wine?" He smirks, raising a brow.

"Oh, I love it. I'm just trying to figure out how you knew

exactly what wine I like." I sip from my glass again, the liquid pooling warmth within me.

"Like I said the other day, Lucy. I know you better than you think."

"How? The same way that you could tell how *wet* I was?" The second glass of wine gives me courage to voice the things I wouldn't normally say and I lean forward, my knee brushing against his.

It might be a trick of the firelight, but his eyes seem to darken, his nostrils flaring. "Something like that."

I'm starting to resent those words. But it doesn't matter right now. Not when there is fire pooling in my belly and his gaze makes me want to rip my clothes off. Baring all for him to claim.

"Tell me," I say, setting my now empty wine glass on the side table, "how does that little trick of yours work?"

"Trick?"

"Is it the way my cheeks flush? Or maybe the way I'm breathing?" I lean in closer. "Or maybe it's the way my body seems to burn up when—"

He closes the distance between us, covering his mouth with mine as he devours me with frenzied hunger. Wrapping my arms around his neck, my breath hitches when he pulls me into his lap so I'm straddling him. The soft swirl of my hips grinding my core against him causes him to moan into my mouth. I want him. God, do I want him and from the grip he has on me and the possessive growl escaping his throat, he wants me to.

"Wait." I force myself to pull away, breathing heavily, realizing we never talked about what happened the other night. The last thing I want is for him to get the wrong idea. I may be a lot of things, but playing with someone's emotions isn't something I'm willing to do. "You said—"

"Forget what I said." He almost growls at me, threading his fingers through the hair at the nape of my neck as he pulls my mouth back down to his.

Well, don't mind if I do.

Our tongues twirl together, and this time he's the one who gently bites my bottom lip as I gasp, grinding down on him once again. Abruptly, he stands, still holding me, and walks to the bedroom. Only once we reach the bed, does he lay me down, untangling himself from me, to reach down and pull off my leggings.

Throwing my sweater over my head, I relish the way his eyes darken further as he takes in my matching black lace panties and bra. "Naughty girl," he murmurs, leaning down to kiss me as I reach to unbutton his pants.

I'd be a complete fucking liar if I said I wasn't hoping this would happen tonight.

He pulls his sweater and shirt off, leaving me to appreciate him in nothing but his boxer briefs. The outline of his thick cock causes my eyes to widen. I haven't even seen it yet, and already I'm trying to understand how it will fit. He doesn't really give me time to appreciate it before he's over me once more.

Slowly, he snakes his hand down the front of my panties, his fingers expertly finding my clit. As he rubs slow, tantalizing circles around the sensitive nub until all I can do is whimper into his mouth. He moves to insert one finger, then another, and slowly fucks me with his fingers while his kisses me.

"You're so wet for me," he whispers. Thrusting in and out, warmth pooling at my core, I clench around his fingers. Excitement fills me as I feel myself growing closer and closer to the edge.

That is, until he suddenly withdraws from my body, while I whimper in protest.

"Patience," he breathes, leaving open mouth kisses trailing down along my neck, down my chest, as he expertly unhooks my bra with one hand, helping me disentangle from it. Only then does another low rumble escape him as his mouth latches onto my firm erect nipple, my back arching as a gasp escapes me.

"Fuck—" I moan, trying my best not to lose myself at the way he makes me feel when he touches me. Everything about this man is primal. A possession that makes my body alight with a burning fire I didn't know existed.

Moving his mouth back to mine, I'm vaguely aware of him removing his boxer-briefs, nestling his head at my entrance. "Are you ready?" he asks, his forehead against mine. My body tenses for a moment as I nod.

"I'm on the pill." A slight rumble sounds in his chest as he gently pushes into me, stretching me so wide I can barely stand it.

Damn, just how big is he?

"I'm sorry if it hurts."

"Someone's quite confident," I grind out, willing my body to get used to the sheer size of him. I could tell before he was big from the outline of him through his boxers, but god, I didn't realize just how big.

He grins as he withdraws slowly, only to reenter to the hilt once again. After a moment of him slowly thrusting into me, all the tightness is replaced by pure pleasure. I can't get enough of him. In fact, I'm not getting enough. He picks up the pace, relentlessly driving into me as my feet hook behind his waist.

"Deeper," I cry out my nails digging into his back.

"Deeper?" He pulls out, flipping me over so I'm on my hands and knees. "I'll fucking give you deeper." He lines himself up with me again, and this time when he enters, I at least know what to expect. I'm lucky I don't have any neighbors because I damn near scream when he plunges all the way in, the tip of his dick perfectly hitting my G spot.

"Oh my god!" I scream, shoving my face into the mattress.

"None of that," he growls, pulling my body up so my back is against his chest. "Let me hear you, Lucy."

My arm reaches behind me to wrap around his neck as he pounds into me from behind, each thrust driving me closer and closer to the edge. His hand moves across my stomach, reaching down to stroke my clit.

Harder and harder he strokes me until finally I break, my pleasure releasing from me in waves that never seem to end. My cries leave my throat feeling raw. Releasing his neck, I lean forward as he continues to drive into me, almost brutally now, until he reaches a point where the thickness of him seems to grow harder and he pulls out, leaving me panting as the sounds of him coming undone echo behind me.

I would have figured he cum inside me since I said I was on the pill. But he doesn't. Perhaps that's simply his preference?

Regardless, my mind is blown from the entire experience.

Collapsing on the bed, I pay him no attention as I hear him move towards the small sink in the room before crawling on the bed next to me. His arms wrap around me, pulling me close to him, my head gently resting on his chest.

"This may not be the best thing to say right now..." Elijah's voice trails off.

"Then don't say it," I yawn, ready to ignore my problems until tomorrow.

"I just realized we just had sex in your dead dad's bed."

"Elijah!" I playfully smack his chest and sit up. "Why would you say that?"

He lifts his hands in a show of surrender. "Hey, it's not that bad. I mean, you changed the sheets, right?"

Rolling my eyes, I lay back down on him. "Yeah, I changed the sheets."

He pulls me to him once more, and lays a kiss to the top of my head that makes me smile. I never imagined coming up here that I'd meet someone. Or that I'd even survive this place. I suppose a part of me wondered if I even could. But now, I don't know what to expect.

"I think my dad might have been crazy," I admit softly. My mind turns over everything that I've learned about my father in the journals I read.

"Why do you say that?"

"He mentioned something about werewolves in some journals that I found. Which is crazy..." His body stiffens, causing me to sit up and look at him. "What?"

"I just...why would that make him crazy?"

I don't try to stifle my laugh. "Maybe because werewolves don't exist?"

Before he can answer, the sound of wolves howling cuts through the air. Elijah stiffens, then jumps out of bed, and immediately looks out the window. "Has that happened before?"

"What, the wolves?" I ask incredulously.

What has gotten him so worked up?

"Yes, Lucy, the wolves," he says urgently, still looking out the window, "I need you to tell me, has this happened before?"

Shaking my head, I scramble for an answer, "I— I mean yes. Every night since I've moved in." He doesn't answer as I get out of bed, putting a hand on his arm. "Elijah, what—"

He looks down at me, something akin to fear in his eyes.

"The wolves are descending."

Chapter 8

Wolf Whisperer

Elijah

Fuck.

"The wolves are descending." The words are out of my mouth before I can think better of it, and I become vaguely aware of the presence of wolves I don't recognize approaching the cabin. Shit. This is not good. My wolf growls under my skin, angry at the danger our mate is in.

"What the fuck does that mean?" Lucy exclaims, scrambling out of the bed, rushing to pull her clothes back on. As much as I mourn losing the sight of her naked body, I don't protest. Not when we are probably about to be overrun by rogues.

"It means..." I say, turning to look at her. And as if looking at her as if for the first time, I truly see her. The waves of her hair, the vibrant green of her eyes. The curve of her lips. My beautiful, strong, fiercely independent mate who has already been through so much in her life. "It means we need to get ready."

Do I really want to bring her into this before she actually loves me? The sound of another howl cutting through the air tells me that it's not my choice anymore.

When I had gone back to my pack, my sister nearly knocked me upside the head when I told her about the fight Lucy and I had. "You idiot!" She had nearly screamed at me. "She may feel an attraction towards you, but at the end of the day, she's human. She isn't bound to the will of the Moon Goddess as we are."

I wasn't a huge fan of the whole smacking me on the head thing, but appreciated the honesty. It feels like almost nobody is honest with me anymore. Besides, if her chastising came from a place of disrespect, I might have had to put her in her place. Even without the Alpha Aura. But, I know that my sister loves me and is genuinely rooting for me to not only find my mate so I can fully become the Alpha, but to fall in love as well.

My heart had panged at the thought of Lucy not feeling the exact same pull I experienced, but...I decided I would make her fall for me. By the time we fall in love, she will accept the whole 'werewolf' thing with open arms.

That might be wishful thinking.

That had earned an eye roll from Bailey, but at least she didn't hit me upside the head again.

Fucking sisters.

There's a sound of banging on the front door that seems to alarm Lucy as it alarms me.

Dammit. They're trying to get in the house.

"Aren't you going to get dressed?" Lucy asks as she finishes pulling on her leggings, motioning to my still naked body.

Shaking my head, I reach my senses out to try to discern just how many rogues we'd be facing. "No, it'll slow me down."

Six rogues. Three by the front door, the other three circling the cabin, either trying to scare us or look for a way in.

Angry at me for not shifting to protect our mate, my wolf scratches at my skin, howling to be let loose. *Not until absolutely necessary,* I tell him. *The others might make it in time to drive them off,* but that only earns a growl from him.

The wolf side of me is irrational. It's all I can do to keep him from completely taking over since he thinks I'm not doing my job well enough.

She looks rightfully baffled. "How the hell would clothing slow you down? And slow you down for what?"

Ignoring the question I'm not ready to answer, I turn back towards the bedroom window. "Lucy, I need you to tell me exactly what's been happening when you hear the howls." If they've been watching her, then they've seen me, and knew I'd be here.

This is all my fucking fault. Though a part of me wonders if this has more to do with her dad than it does with me. I checked with the Elders when I got back to the pack, and there was a human doctor who was employed by the pack living in this cabin. They couldn't tell me why we would employ a human doctor, just that my father had been interested in his research. If my father was interested in the research, it couldn't have been anything good.

She blanches a moment, then shakes her head. "I don't understand—"

"Lucy. Please. What's been happening?"

"I...the first night, I heard howling all night. Then the next night, after you left, I saw two wolves watching me from the treeline—"

"What color were their eyes?" It doesn't matter, I already know the answer. But I need to hear it from her.

"Um, red? I think? But—"

My wolf growls again. Red eyes. Definitely rogues.

Quickly mindlinking my pack, I send out the message. *"Riftan, I need you. Rogue attack at my mate's cabin. Bring Bailey and our strongest warriors. I sense 6 rogues outside."*

His answer is quick. *"We are on our way, Alpha"*

I've been leading the pack for years, but I'm not technically the Alpha, not yet. Unbeknownst to the rest of us, years before his death, my dad requested that the Elders put a stipulation on the transfer of the Alpha Aura. As a result, the Elders hold a bind on the Aura until the condition is met. That condition being me taking a mate, fated or not. Nobody knew what his motivation was at the time, but even though the Elders didn't agree with his decision, they were powerless to do anything but what he commanded.

Alpha Aura or not, I will never rule with the fear my father did.

"Dammit, Lucy! Why wouldn't you say anything?" I'm angry, the emotions from my wolf side bleeding into my voice. But I'm not angry at her. Not when I should have sensed these rogues sooner. If I was truly the Alpha, I would have been able to sense them from a mile away. But no, my shit dad had to screw me over in just one more way when he died.

My wolf howls angrily. *Yeah, I'm pissed too.*

"I don't understand, Elijah." Her voice shakes as she peered out the window. "I'm scared. What's going on?"

"I"m sorry. You wouldn't have known." Turning to Lucy, I grasp her upper arms with my hands. "Everything is going to be alright. Help is on the way."

Her brows furrow, as she sits, perching herself on the edge of the bed. "What help? Are you an actual cop or something? Are cops even trained to handle rabid wolves?"

My mouth nearly drops open. "Rabid wolves…? No, they aren't rabid wolves." Shaking my head, I move closer to the door of the bedroom. "It's hard to explain, but you aren't safe here by yourself anymore." The sound of the banging grows louder each time, like the sturdiness of the door only angers the rogues, making them more and more determined to knock it down.

As I move toward the open bedroom door to attempt to see the front door, Lucy speaks up. "If they aren't rabid wolves, then what are they? What if we just tossed some raw meat out the window? Will they go away?" She's tapping her finger against her leg nervously, a habit I would find adorable under normal circumstances. "Maybe they're just hungry." A part of me admires her problem-solving spirit, she'll make a perfect Luna. But for now, I really wish she would just take my word for it.

"They're not hungry," I say matter-of-factly.

"How could you possibly know that? Do you think you're some kind of wolf-whisperer or something?"

"Or something," I answer, not looking away from the door and I know she's sick and tired of my cryptic answers. I don't know how I"m going to keep this from her at this rate. Why the fuck are the rogues *here*, and how did they know about Lucy?

"Where the fuck are you, Riftan?!" I mindlink again, desperate for a way for this to all go away before I have to expose Lucy to the truth.

"We're coming, Eli. Rogues were waiting for us just outside the pack borders, like they knew you would call for us," Riftan answers.

Shit. This whole thing was planned, and I was so focused on wooing Lucy, I didn't even see it. First thing I'll do after Lucy lets me claim her is hunt down the Rogue Alpha and rip his fucking throat out. Physically, he's on the same level as I am, since he doesn't have an Alpha Aura either. His pack is made up of deserters and rejects, evident by the red of their eyes that manifests due to the severing of the pack bond.

The front door violently shakes with each assault, so hard I think it might be ripped off its hinges at any second. The sound of angry wolves snarling is muffled behind the door. Apparently they hadn't expected the door to be so sturdy.

My wolf itches to break free, but he also wants to comfort our mate. Shaking my head, I walk towards her and take hold of her hands. "I need you to trust me. Please. I promise I'm going to protect you, but I also promise that things are going to get a hell of a lot more scary before they get better." She says nothing, her eyes widening a fraction before I continue, "I need you to stay in here. No matter what you hear, no matter what you see. Can you promise me that?"

"What are you—"

Abruptly, I stand, darting down the hall to grab a fire poker from next to the hearth, hoping to hell she won't have to use it. But six rogues against just me? I may be stronger than each of them individually as the heir to the Alpha line, but taking all of them at once? That whole not-having-the-Alpha-Aura thing is really fucking with me right now.

Resuming my place in front of her, I shove the poker into her hands, ignoring her shocked expression as I tell her, "if anyone comes in here, you use this. You don't ask questions. Whether they're wolf," I swallow, daring to meet her eyes, "or human. Your life is the most precious thing in this godforsaken place. If they have the same tattoo as me, they're safe. But if you feel like you're in danger, please stab them."

The thought of Lucy having to protect herself from anything sends my wolf into a spiral. *We* should be protecting her.

But we are, I tell myself, it's safer for her if we face the rogues as far from her as possible. And if the others don't get here soon…

My wolf growls. We will not be defeated.

"What…" She looks down at me, concern in her gaze. "You're insane.

Grimacing, I stand. "I almost wish that were the case."

For a moment, the banging against the door stops. Lucy lets out a sigh of relief, setting the fire poker down. "See, they're gone. They probably just went somewhere else."

The sound of glass shattering makes her jump up, and her trembling hands grasp mine desperately. Her face pales as the sound of growling wolves echoing down the hall into the room.

I wish we had more time before she found out. I wish she had fallen in love with me before this happened. I don't know how I'll convince her to stay now.

"Remember, stay here." Gently removing her hands from mine, I shove the fire poker back into her hands before stepping toward the door. Speechless, she watches as I step into the hallway, willing my features to convey just how sorry I am.

"I'm going in," I mindlink Riftan.

"We're almost there!" His voice echoes in my mind, but I can't afford to wait any longer. Lucy could get hurt if I do.

Blocking out the sounds of the snarling rogues just in the other room, I hold Lucy's gaze letting out a heavy breath. "Your dad wasn't crazy."

And without breaking eye contact, I let out my wolf.

Chapter 9

No Ass Cheeks on the Furniture

Lucy

A gigantic, black wolf stares at me from where Elijah had been only a moment before. He turns his head towards the intruders and launches himself down the hall. I might be screaming. It's so hard to tell over the sound of wolven teeth gnashing together and angry snarls.

Elijah just turned into a wolf.
Like, an actual fucking wolf.

I can't believe I just slept with a literal beast, who could *literally* tear me limb from limb if he felt so inclined. I mean, I've done some dumb shit in my life but this tops it all.

Gripping the fire poker tightly, I step hesitantly toward the bedroom door. Remembering Elijah's urging to stay in the room. As much as I want to listen to him, to trust in what he's saying—should I?

You know what? No. Fuck him. Fuck him and this ridiculous secret he kept from me.

Peering around the open doorway, I cringe as I hear crashing, the wolves clearly having no regard for my personal effects. Slowly, I step down the hallway, sighing as I realize that Elijah has managed to move the fight outside. My living room is completely trashed though.

Crawling on the floor, fire poker still in hand, I move on my hands and knees until I reach the window that looks out to the front yard. Elijah is facing six of those wolves all on his own.

I'm sure it's Elijah, he's the only wolf with black fur out there, and an unwelcome surge of pride fills my chests as I observe that he's the largest wolf out there. If he were standing next to me, his head would be about level with my shoulder. The other wolves would probably come up to my ribcage, and have some variation of brown fur, their eyes red.

You can't be impressed with a dog, Lucy.

Blinking, I shake my head. Right. This is over now. Now that I know he's a wolf, this thing is done.

Never thought that *would be a sentence I would say.*

Despite my internal claim of not wanting to be involved with him anymore, my heart catches when one of the wolves throws themselves at him. He's ready though, and uses the momentum of their jump to grab the scruff of its neck, and throws it into a nearby tree. The wolf hits the tree with a thud, a whimper escaping it as it lays at the base. The three remaining wolves close in, filling the empty space the one attacked had left behind.

Three...? That means that he's already taken half of them out by himself.

Howls in the distance cause bile to turn in my gut. Fuck. Would he be able to handle more enemies? What if they come for me next?

A blur of red launches itself at one of the wolves surrounding Elijah, and snarling and yipping escapes the tangle of brown and red causing relief to fill my chest. His words echo in my mind, *"help is on the way,"* Right. Did this mean that he had influence over other wolves since he could turn into one?

Before I can contemplate further, another black blur, about three quarters the size of Elijah, attacks a larger brown wolf, with the help of a gray wolf. Growls and snarls fill the air, Elijah taking on the last wolf himself.

I must be dreaming. But I've never had a dream this *vivid* before. It must be the wine. And the orgasm. I probably fell asleep after telling Elijah about my dad and the werewolves, and the hormones running wild in my body have reduced me to a hyper-realistic, super terrifying, werewolf attack dream.

Yes, that had to be it. There was no other way to explain this. As I watch Elijah return to human form, I can't help but scan his body for any injuries. Call it second nature, or what...I can't help but worry he's hurt. That is until the other wolves with him begin to also transform into human forms, and I feel my heart sinking.

"No fucking way..."

Not only are they like Elijah, but they're all fucking naked.

What the fuck. They're all actually human too? What the fuck is this...there's no way this is real. Werewolves don't exist!

The sight of Elijah stalking back toward the cabin has me scrambling, backing into a corner like some kind of terrified animal, cornered by a predator.

"Lucy," he breathes out, after stepping into the cabin. His eyes fall on me in the corner of the room. "I told you to—"

"Get the fuck away from me." My teeth are clenched, fire poker pointing outward. Gone was the sweet man I saw myself *maybe* falling in love with someday, replaced by a literal monster who had deceived me in every sense. Who had *slept* with me, for fuck's sake.

My arms shake as he takes another step forward, his hands raised in surrender. "Lucy, I know that was a lot to take in—"

"*A lot to take in?!*" My voice is almost a screech as a near delirious cackle leaves my throat. Keeping the fire poker pointed in front of me, I move so my back is to the kitchen, and from this view, I can see four naked humans slowly stepping toward the cabin, three men, one woman. "Talk about understatement of the year, Elijah," a tormented thought occurs to me, "Is your name even Elijah?"

He sighs, taking a step toward me, as if trying to calm a petulant child. "Of course my name is Elijah, Lucy. Come on, be reasonable here."

"Reasonable?! You turned into a fucking wolf!" I screech at him, arms shaking as I stare at him in horror. "Take another step and I'll put this fire poker straight through your fucking throat."

"Lucy." His voice is soft, a plea. That's quickly dismissed as movement behind him catches my eye.

"I like her," the only woman of the group exclaims, smiling at me. "She's gonna make you work for it." Against my will, feelings of jealousy bloom in my chest at the sight of another woman touching him. Even if it's just her hand upon his shoulder.

"Not helping, Bailey."

"Bailey...your sister?" My voice wavers slightly, the fire poker lowering an inch.

A grin breaks out on her face and I notice the similarities between the two of them. Both have strong, athletic builds, straight noses, high cheekbones, same blue eyes. "Twin sister, actually," she says, reaching out a hand. Like she wants me to shake it. Like she isn't standing in my living room, naked as the day she was born, blood on her cheek from battle with insidious wolves which now that I think about, can probably turn into humans too.

"I—" My eyes dart down to her hand, my fire poker lowering slightly more. "He said you were his little sister."

"You asshole." She turns, punching him in the shoulder, earning a grimace from him. Turning back to me, she sighs. "Yeah, he loves flaunting that he was born three minutes before me."

Before I can stop myself, I feel a grin slide its way on my face. I think I could like this girl...wolf. Whatever she is. Deciding that dropping the fire poker is the best course of action, I place it back at its place on the hearth, and turn back towards Elijah and Bailey.

"Can I...explain?" His voice is hesitant.

"You lied, Elijah, what is there to explain? Not only that, but you brought chaos into my home, you're a...you're a fucking wolf."

"Shifter—" he corrects me, but then shakes his head. "Listen, I know you're upset. I know you feel like I lied to you—"

"Because you did."

"I withheld the truth. Because," he sighs, "let's be real here. You had just met me, I was in your cabin. If I had said, 'oh yeah, by the way, I'm a wolf,' would have even believed me?"

Pursing my lips, I play through what that would have looked like in reality. "I probably would have either thought you were insane, or have a really terrible sense of humor," I admit.

He's right. I would have laughed him right out the front door.

He takes one more ill-advised step. "Can I please explain?"

"Fine." I'll allow it...for now.

"Can we come in too?" the redhead calls from outside. "My ass cheeks are starting to freeze."

Begrudgingly, I allow them in. "No ass cheeks on the furniture, I don't care how frozen they are," I call out as they file inside the cabin. Elijah goes to retrieve blankets from the armoire in my room to put on the furniture. I'm in the armchair, warily eyeing one of the naked men, er, warriors, as Elijah had said, when Bailey comes into the room with a cup of steaming tea.

"Thank you," I murmur, taking the cup from her gratefully.

Elijah settles on the couch, his clothes now on, thank goodness. Before he turns to Bailey. "Okay where should we start?"

"The fuck if I know." She shrugs, taking a seat next to the redhead. "Maybe ask if she has any questions?"

Turning to me, his eyes soften. "Do you have any questions?"

"Um, yeah, I do." I shift in my seat, careful not to spill my tea. "Were those other wolves werewolves too? Do we know why they were attacking me?"

Elijah nods. "Yes, they were also *shifters*. They're called rogues. But we don't know why they targeted you."

I nod, taking in the information, not missing how he's

corrected me twice now. Not werewolves, shifters. I take a moment trying to remember if I had changed in front of an open window the last few days. Deciding to ask my next question, I go with the obvious. "Why is everyone still naked?"

Bailey chokes on a laugh.

He rubs the back of his neck. "Nudity is not as taboo in the pack as it is in human culture."

The pack?

Oh right, that's what he said in his note, that he had to go run his pack. "Why?" I ask, more curious now.

"We shift—er, can turn into wolves. From the time that we're teens. We shift so often, and the clothes rip if we shift while wearing them. Not to mention, it's next to impossible to make sure that clothes are readily available if we have to shift back to human form while off the territory." He shrugs. "It's normal to us because it's a necessity. We weren't raised to think of it as strange, so we don't."

I suppose that makes sense. That doesn't make *me* any more comfortable with it, though. "Fair enough." I nod, taking in everything around me. "I still can't get over how everyone is just acting so normal, so unbothered and making tea when you were just a wolf ripping out someone's throat."

"Hey now, nobody's throat was *actually* ripped out," Bailey pipes up, raising a brow.

"That being said..." Elijah gives her what I can only interpret as a warning look. "We can act normal because this is our normal, for the Alpha, Beta, and Warriors, anyway. Others in the pack might be more shaken up, but for us, it's just another Tuesday."

"Alpha? Beta?" I shake my head. "I don't know what any of that means."

"Pack semantics." Elijah brushes off the question. "We have plenty of time to get you familiar with all the terms. I promise you Lucy, I will help you adjust to this life."

Help me adjust...?

"No." I shake my head, realizing what he means. "No. You

think..." an incredulous laugh escapes me, "you think I'm going to be a part of *this life?*"

Elijah's expression is concentrated for a moment, and without another word, all the other werewolves stand up and file into the kitchen.

I swallow nervously as he gets up from his space on the couch, on his knees before me, just like he was before the wolves got into the house.

"Lucy." Giving me a pleading gaze, he stares up at me . "I know you're scared, and I can't blame you. But..." He closes his eyes a moment, before opening them again, his eyes clear. "You belong with me, Lulu. You feel it, don't you?" He reaches for my hands, and before I can stop myself, before I know if I even would have stopped myself, my hands jerk away, my eyes wide, my heart pumping rapidly in my chest.

I'm finding out that I really don't know much of anything, but I know that I've deeply hurt the man I was starting to care for. He withdraws his hands, turning from me. "You should get some sleep. I'll guard the rest of the house."

Before I can say anything else, he's gone. Disappeared from the doorway and vanished to do what he said he was going to do. The soft sound of the others in the kitchen whispering to each other, the only noise that lets me know everything that has happened, was real.

And despite the fact that there are so many people currently in my home, I feel alone. The torment of approaching sleep weighs heavily on me. Promising my nightmares that are sure to come.

Chapter 10

I'm an Atheist

Lucy

Stretching my arms over my head, I sit up in bed and blearily look around my bedroom. Not a hair out of place, it seems. There is, however, a steaming mug of coffee on my bedside table, complete with the creamer Elijah had brought with him.

Damn, that was a weird dream.

Sipping on my coffee, I wonder where Elijah's gone off to. My stomach gurgles with hunger and the realization that I need to eat. He did leave me this coffee, maybe he's the type to make breakfast the next morning too. Changing my clothes, I chuckle and shake my head at my dream the night before. Werewolves. The very thought makes me feel ridiculous.

The moment I step over to the small bathroom attached to the house, I turn on the faucet and it only barely runs with water causing my brows to furrow. "What the hell?"

I know when I came up here there was water…why is it barely working now?

One more thing I have to worry about.

Giving up on the notion for now, I decide to seek out Elijah. Perhaps, he'll know exactly what's going on with the water. God knows the man knows how to sort everything else. As I make my way towards the kitchen passing the living room, something catches my eye.

Whipping my head around, I scan the room, but find nothing out of place, except for a stack of folded blankets on the armchair. *Hmmm.* My eyes dart to a window that's been covered by brown butcher paper, a hole in the corner letting the chill in from outside.

No.

The sound of low murmuring coming from the kitchen makes me stop in my tracks. Not just one voice but multiple voices. A female one as well.

No.

No no no no...maybe if I go back to bed, I can try again. Try again to wake up to a normal, average, werewolf-free life. I take a step backward, ready to quickly retreat from the hallway.

"Lucy!" Bailey exclaims, fully clothed as she smiles at me from the kitchen doorway, a frying pan in her hand. "Come on over! Breakfast is just about ready."

Reality quickly catches up to me, and I relive the events from the day before not as if they were the dream I had convinced myself of just moments before, but actual real life.

Fuck. There goes all hope for a peaceful day.

Swallowing, I nod as Bailey disappears back into the kitchen, tentatively following behind her, the sound of voices grow slightly louder. There's no way this is real. It can't be.

The moment I reach the entryway, I allow my body to lean against it as I observe the scene in front of me. They're all sitting around my kitchen table, talking in low voices. Elijah, the redhead, and a gray-haired man are all sitting down with two empty seats at the table, and I watch as Bailey chimes in periodically while putting plates of scrambled eggs, bacon, and toast at the table's center.

My stomach rumbles again, causing all four people to look in my direction.

"Hungry?" Bailey raises a brow, lifting the pan in her hand.

"My stomach wasn't that loud," I mutter, going to sit on the chair that's not directly next to Elijah. Hurt flashes across his face before he helps himself to some eggs.

"Shifter hearing," the one with gray hair explains, a sheepish grin on his face, "I'm Laurent."

"Hi, Laurent." I nod my head, noting that despite his full head of gray hair, he couldn't have been older than thirty.

"Since we're doing introductions," the redhead speaks-up, "I'm Riftan, Eli's Beta."

"Hi, Riftan," I smile, putting some toast on my plate. "I'm sorry…Beta? What does that mean?"

Bailey elbows Riftan's shoulder. "Yeah, dummy. She doesn't know what any of this means yet."

I have to keep myself from smiling at Bailey. If we had met under different circumstances, I would have wanted her to be my friend.

"Ugh." Riftan rubs his shoulder, wincing. "Beta…basically like a second in command."

I gulp, finally letting my gaze slide to Elijah. "So you're…first in command?"

"Unofficially." He grimaces, taking a sip of coffee.

"And obviously, I'm Bailey. The best breakfast cook in the state of Alaska," Bailey chimes in, with a grin on her face.

"Gotcha," I try to act like everything is normal. Like there aren't four werewolves eating breakfast in my kitchen like it's just any other day.

"Are you okay?" Elijah asks, as if I would be after everything that happened.

"Not really…but, I do have a question."

His eyes light up, as his gorgeous smile lines his face. "Anything…what is it?"

"Can you…look at the water? It's acting like something's wrong."

They all pause, a look of confusion on their face until Bailey turns the kitchen sink on and watches as the water only trickles out. "The reserve must be low..."

"Reserve?"

"Yeah," Elijah states chiming in from Baily's comment. "This is a dry cabin. You're not hooked up to a regular water line. Most people with dry cabins have water reserves that they have to replenish every week or so. I saw your dad's the other day when I was chopping wood, but I didn't check the levels. It's large, but I'm sure with you taking a shower and other things, it's depleted."

Great. Now I have to figure out how to fix that as well.

"Thanks, I'll have to find a way to get some from town."

After an awkward moment of silence, Elijah clears his throat. "Listen, Lucy...it's not safe for you to be here by yourself anymore."

My heart drops. "What do you mean?"

"The rogues...the ones who attacked us last night, they were here the night I was gone, right?"

I nodded numbly, not comforted by the fact that I was lucky they waited until Elijah was here to attack.

"We believe that they will continue to come, whether I'm here or not. And, I know that you do not wish for me to be here anymore...so I can't keep you safe." He swallows and stares at me, as if he's waiting for me to refute his last statement.

"Do we know why they keep coming here? What draws them to this cabin?" My throat is dry. So, so dry that I can hardly concentrate. "I didn't even know about..." I make myself choke out the word, "werewolves, until last night."

Elijah silently pushes a glass of water to me before answering. "We don't know. The only connection is me."

"So you're the reason they're coming here," I state, meeting his gaze evenly.

"It's more complicated than that—"

"I don't think it's that complicated at all actually. I'm not leaving," I say with finality, "This is your fault." I point my fork at him. "You showed up at *my* door, while I was just trying to write my book and live in peace. You say the only connection is you. If that's the case, if you stop coming around here, so will they. Am I right in assuming that you had a run in with these rogues the night before you showed up on my porch?"

Grimly, he nods, and I continue, "then, they only hung around after you left to see if you'd come back, which you did."

"That's not—"

I hold up my hand, stopping him mid sentence. "Once a couple of days have passed, they'll see that you are nowhere to be found, they will move on with their lives, leaving me in peace." I nod, satisfied with my conclusion. However, as positive as I was about my conclusion, the looks the others give me afterwards makes me doubt myself.

"That won't work," Riftan says, chewing his toast.

Frowning, I look at him. "Why not?"

"Ask him." He points to Elijah.

"Why won't it work?"

"Because I can't just leave it to chance that they won't show up." He sighs, still being very tight-lipped with his response. There's clearly something that he isn't telling me and the more he keeps hiding things, the less I want him and the others to be here.

"Why not, Elijah?" I ask again, slightly more annoyed than before. "You just met me, I mean nothing to you."

"It's not up to me, I need to keep you safe, even my wolf—"

"Your wolf? Fuck that, I'm not here to talk about wolfy things. There's no reason you can't just—"

"Fuck, Lucy! It's because you're my mate!" His voice echoes throughout the room, and in the following silence, anyone could hear a pin drop.

"I'm your...*mate*?" I ask in disbelief. "What the hell is a mate? Like, Australian for 'friend' kind of thing..." I look around the table at grim faces. "Right?"

He sighs, rubbing his temple. "It's a *wolf thing*. A ridiculous fate thing. I feel a...pull when I'm with you. A spark. A gift from the Moon Goddess. It's designed to help shifters find the perfect partner for them."

He's fucking joking, right?

Shaking my head, my voice wavers, "I am no such thing. I would...I would know."

"But don't you?" He gets up, walks around the table, and grabs my hand before I can pull away. I try to fight the thrill of excitement that flows up my arm. "Don't you feel this?"

"What I feel..." I reply, snatching my hand away, "is a result of my hormones raging out of control at the touch of a moderately attractive man after not having sex for five months."

He shakes his head. "No, the Moon Goddess—"

"I'm an atheist." I snap. "So you can tell this 'Moon Goddess' to just back the fuck off and stay out of my life."

"She's not bound to the whims of the Moon Goddess as we are," Bailey says, earning murmurs of agreement from Riftan and Laurent. "She's not going to understand."

"Your goddess messed up," I reply quickly. "I'm just a human. How can a human be a 'perfect partner' for a...a..."

"Alpha," Riftan pipes up.

"Right," I answer as Elijah gives him a dirty look. "How can a human be a perfect match for an Alpha? I...I didn't ask for any of this."

Elijah's face turns hard. "Well, tough luck, Lucy. It's sealed in stone. Now that I've had you, I can never have another. Everyone at this table," he motions to everyone in the room, "can *smell* the fact that we've already slept together. Our scents have merged. That means that the rogues can smell it too." My cheeks flame in embarrassment at his words, my eyes avoiding Riftan, Laurent, and Bailey altogether.

How *dare* he?

"A decision that I am coming to deeply regret," I hiss at him.

A flash of hurt strikes his eyes before his expression goes cold. "I told you that once you sleep with me, then you're mine forever. Do you remember that?" Gritting my teeth, I nod. "That's what I meant. These are the consequences we face. I have to keep you safe, and this is how I keep you safe. You're coming with me."

"I don't belong to you," I reply, standing from the table. "I didn't ask for any of this. I'm staying here. I'm sorry that I'm your mate. I truly am. I feel for you. But I don't accept any of this, it's *my* life, and I'm deciding that I'm not going."

"Lucy." He makes one last pleading face at me. "You've lost everyone you love. This is a chance...a chance to have a family. Not just me, but everyone in the pack. I will be their Alpha, and in turn, you will be their *Luna*. You will lead with me. It won't matter that you're human. The bond of the fated mate is more sacred to shifters than anything in the entire world."

I thought about his words for a moment. Didn't I always want to belong to a family? A place where I wasn't just tolerated, but *wanted*...needed? His gaze is hopeful as I chew my lip, thinking how I'll answer him. As much as I want to say yes, I can't.

"Listen, Elijah, that sounds great. But...I can't. I'm not going. I have to find out more about dad and—"

A growl escapes him as he grabs me, throwing me over his shoulder like a sack of flour. "What the *fuck!?*" I shriek as I bang my fists as hard as I can on his back, but it doesn't even phase him. "Put me down, *right fucking now*!" I have never been so pissed in my entire life. The rage that fills me nearly lights my skin on fire.

He turns, and I catch glimpses of Riftan, Laurent, and Bailey's horrified faces. I kick with all my might, hoping he catches a foot in the face. "Sorry, Lucy," he says, his voice irritated. "If you're going to act like a child about this whole thing, then I'm going to have to treat you like one."

"A child?!" My voice reaches a new pitch as I continue to bang on his back, scratching where I can. "Fuck you, asshole! Put me the fuck down, Elijah!"

"Elijah..." Riftan's voice is quiet, and I see him place a hand on Elijah's arm. Would he be able to talk some sense into him and tell him how barbaric this is?

"Don't," he snarls, jerking his arm away, jostling me in the process. "This is my order as Alpha." A muscle tics in Riftan's jaw before he nods, taking a step back.

How the hell they can hear him over the noise I'm making is beyond me, but Elijah turns to Bailey. "Pack a bag for her. Bring her father's journals."

"Don't fucking touch my stuff! I'm not going anywhere with you! You…you…rude, brutish, inconsiderate fuck!"

"I'm so sorry, Lucy…" Bailey mutters, her voice uncharacteristically downcast, before she disappears into my room.

It doesn't matter what I say or do. Elijah has set his mind to this and is acting like I have no choice. As if everything I want is completely irrelevant.

"Lucy, you acting like this won't make it any easier."

"What?! You're basically fucking kidnapping me!"

"No, I'm going to claim you. I'm sorry, Lucy, but I can't officially take over my pack until I've found and claimed my fated mate. We're going to have to learn to get along at some point, so don't say something you'll regret later."

"I'll say whatever the fuck I want, dickhead."

He shakes his head in resignation, stepping outside the cabin. While Riftan and Laurent follow quietly behind us, exchanging worried glances. As the door shuts behind us, my scream of rage, the only sound echoing through the empty hills around us.

Chapter 11

Damn, That's Convenient

Lucy

"So, you guys are cool with women being kidnapped out of their homes?" I gave up on pounding on Elijah's back about five minutes in, and now I brace my arms on his back, keeping my head up the best as I can as I shoot death glares at Riftan and Laurent.

Riftan had tossed a blanket on top of me, which did little against the cold, but Elijah's body heat was more than enough to make up for it.

"When the future of the pack depends on it? Unfortunately, yes," he replies, avoiding eye contact with me.

"And you?" I turn my gaze to Laurent. "You're just going to sit here and let him do this to an innocent woman?"

"Even if I wanted to stop him," Laurent eyes me carefully, "which I don't, I must obey my Alpha."

I can't help but raise a brow at his statement. "I thought he was only unofficially the Alpha?" That remark earns me a growl from Elijah that I can feel rumbling in his chest. Which is kind of hot, not that I'll tell him that.

"I have everything but the last step, a stipulation set by my father, that I must be mated before I officially take over as Alpha. However, I still lead the pack. I still have all the responsibilities of Alpha, and I still have everyone's loyalty and respect."

"So..." I muse, "it's kind of like being an intern."

Riftan chokes on a laugh and Laurent's lip turns up slightly. Suddenly, I'm jostled somewhat violently on Elijah as he leaps across something. "Ooof!" My breath escapes me.

"Sorry," Elijah says, not sounding sorry at all, "had to jump over that log back there."

My eyes search for some kind of giant tree fallen in our path, but only see a small log that even I could have stepped over easily.

Asshole.

"Wouldn't this be faster if you guys went all...wolfy?" I ask, tapping my chin.

"It would be," Elijah bristles. "But I don't trust you to not leap off my back and make a run for it."

"Wise decision," I concede, sighing as I look around the snow white plains that surround us, wary of any wolf eyes that might peek out at me. "Soooo," I say, determined to annoy Elijah as much as possible, "what is a Luna?"

Laurent and Riftan exchange a look but then their eyes are glued to the back of Elijah's head. After what feels like a long time, their eyes shift to me, and Riftan starts speaking, "Well—"

"Wait," I interrupt, waving my finger between them and Elijah, "what was that?"

"What was what?" Laurent asks innocently.

"That...you were just staring at the back of Elijah's head instead of answering me."

"Pack mindlink," Elijah mumbles.

Shaking my head, I look between the two werewolves in front of me. "Mindlink? Like...he was talking to you?"

Riftan's eyes focus on Elijah again for a moment, and I feel Elijah nod next to me, like he's giving permission for something.

"The Pack mindlink is primarily designed for when we're in our wolf forms," Riftan explains. "It carries over in our human forms too, and as Alpha, he can speak to all of us even when he's not in wolf form."

Damn, that's convenient.

"So, you two," I motion between Laurent and Riftan with my finger, "can't mindlink now, but you can when you're wolves, but he," I jam my thumb over my shoulder, "can mindlink anyone, any time he wants?"

Laurent nods. "It's a perk of being in the Alpha line, even if he's not," he punctuates the next word with air quotes, "'officially' Alpha."

"What was he saying to you after I asked what a Luna is?"

They exchanged a worried glance, and Elijah speaks behind me. "I told them to only tell you the bare minimum."

"Why is that?"

"Because you're a human who didn't know about the existence of shifters until about twelve hours ago, and this is a lot of new information. Forgive me if I didn't want to overwhelm you."

"Oh, yes, because my poor delicate human brain cannot handle all this information." I roll my eyes, turning my gaze back to Riftan. "You were saying?"

Riftan sighs, then continues, "Luna's are the female partners of the Alpha. The Alpha's job is to protect the pack, make sure defenses are tight, etc. Luna's...they are kind of like the mother of the pack. She is respected, revered, and held in the highest regard. She handles all of the pack's inner workings. Housing and food, inter-pack disputes, politics with other packs..." He trails off at my facial expression.

The expression that says that is the absolute *last* thing I want to do. Instead of stating that though, I ask the question that's been gnawing at me. "Is it...common for a human to become Luna?"

Riftan and Laurent exchange one of those infuriating glaces again, and this time it's Laurent who speaks. "It is...unprecedented. But Alpha Elijah is loved by the pack, and as shifters, we hold the fated mate bond sacred above all else. You *should* be welcomed with open arms." He gives me an indecipherable look. "If the Moon Goddess has chosen you, then there must be a reason," he says, sounding more like he's trying to convince himself than me.

The Moon Goddess can fuck right off.

After what seems like forever, Elijah finally slows as we come over a hill. "We're here," he says roughly. "Can I trust you to not run away if I put you down?"

"Probably not," I say bitterly.

Sighing, he continues walking down the hill, his feet crunching in the snow. Reaching the bottom of the hill, I look down to realize we're walking on ice, and notice that none of the men with me are having any trouble staying upright as we walk on what should be a slippery surface. Ice that could crack and leave me flailing for my life in ice cold waters. My heart lurches in fear, and seeing my expression, Laurent quickly tells me, "It's solid, don't worry. Many children go ice skating on these frozen ponds during the winter."

Swallowing, I nod, but still breathe a sigh of relief when we're back on the snow.

Taking in my surroundings as we continue, it looks like the area is surrounded by a thick wall of trees, but within those treelines are multiple houses, some small cabins, something that looks like a general store, and possibly a doctor's office. I look down in embarrassment as several normal looking people, who I would never peg for werewolves, peer at me with curiosity, and at their Alpha with a woman flung over his shoulder.

"Starting to regret your choice?" Elijah asks lightly.

"Not at all," I grit my teeth. "We've been walking for what I'm guessing is over an hour. So, having you carry me saves me from exhaustion."

Before I know it, we're stepping into a house. The warmth of the home seeps into my skin causing a smile to cross my lips. I can't see much from where I'm at but it looks rather large, and my suspicions are only confirmed as Elijah continues to a flight of stairs that make me jostle as he climbs up them. That has to be... two flights of stairs.

When we enter a bedroom, he unceremoniously dumps me on the bed, then walks back to the door. "This is your room," is all he says as he turns the handle.

Sitting up in a rage, I yell after him. "What, you drag me all the way here and now you're just leaving me?"

He turns, his jaw tight. "I didn't think you would *want* me to stay."

"Well for once, you're right." Crossing my arms, I look up at him. "I hate you."

"Ouch," he deadpans, rolling his eyes. "Hate me all you want, it won't change anything."

"You're wrong about this mate thing. Because there is no way that I could be fated to someone who would *fucking kidnap me* just because he thinks he has some wolfy claim on me!"

"You're so stubborn," he seethes, removing his hand from the doorknob. "I did not kidnap you, I fucking saved your life!" His voice starts to rise and hesitation fills me. "You think I like this? You think I enjoy being fated to someone who doesn't accept me?"

I get a sick sense of satisfaction from his anger. "I think you like having power over people," I snarl. "You may have dragged me here but I will *never* choose you."

"Yeah, well, you're not who I would have picked either, sweetheart."

The sting from his words is like a stab to the heart. As much as I don't want to care that he said what he did, I can't help it. My face softens, as I stare at him like he just slapped me in the face.

Elijah's face scrunches up, as if he's digging into the deepest recesses of his mind just to find a word bad enough to call me. "You're just a...a..."

"A *what*?" My voice is quiet, venomous. Daring him to say what he really thinks to I can tear him a new one.

"A human!" he replies, before slamming my door.

I'm not sure why that offended me so much, or why my heart sank at the sound of my door slamming. But it did. I *am* a human. I wanted him to leave. And yet...

I finally look around the room he's placed me in. The comforter is a beautiful teal, with minimalistic white flowers embroidered over its entirety. To my left there's a TV, a DVD player, a couch in the corner, and a bookshelf. To my right, double french doors that lead out to a balcony. I explore one of the two doors on the wall directly in front of the bed. Tentatively opening the first, I find an open space with shelving and rows of clothing hanging up. Running a hand through the clothes, I notice that they're all my size.

Did he have this done for me?

Opening the next door, my mouth nearly drops at the opulence of the bathroom. Decked out with a claw-footed tub, stone-walled shower, and a wall that is exclusively a mirror, this bathroom is nicer than any I've ever been in, let alone had all to myself. Though, I notice that the shower doesn't seem to have a shower head. Curious, I walk over, turning on the water. The water falls from the ceiling as if it's raining, and my eyes grow in surprise.

This is really fucking nice.

"Lucy?" Someone calls my name from the other room, and I'm half tempted to shut the bathroom door and lock myself in, but it sounds like it might be Bailey, so I poke my head out.

"Oh, there you are." She smiles warmly, her arms full of my clothes and my father's journals. "Where do you want all this?"

"Did you carry that all the way here?" I rush to grab some of the stuff from her. "We can just toss it on the bed for now. Thank you though...for doing that."

"It's fine." She shrugs. "It wasn't that bad."

"Still..." I bite my lip feeling more and more guilty about everything that's happened since I met her. Part of me wants to hate them, but the other part of me can't.

"Lucy, really, I'm good." She smiles brightly at me, and despite my upset state, I can't help but return it.

Suddenly, her stance becomes awkward, and quickly she tucks a strand of hair behind her ear. "Listen...I'm sorry. I'm sorry that he brought you here against your will." Just as quickly as she had gotten serious, a grin replaces her grimace as she grabs my hands excitedly. "And I know Eli can be an asshole. But give it time."

Tears prick at my eyes, and before I can answer, another figure is in the doorway, knocking gently with their knuckles. "Lucy?" a soft, gentle voice calls out.

"Mom." Bailey turns to the figure, dropping my hands to pull her inside. "This is Lucy." She looks at me. "Lucy, this is our mom, current acting Luna of the Blood Moon pack."

I swallow, taking in the woman in front of me. She is only slightly taller than I am, and though you can see the lines of age on her face, her body still seems as fit and strong as her daughter next to her. Their matching sets of piercing blue eyes would be indication enough of their relation, even if she hadn't introduced herself.

"Hi." I force a smile. "I'm Lucy." I reach out my hand, and she grasps it with both of hers.

"Lucy, dear, it's so lovely to meet you. You can call me Sage. I know you were...reluctant to come, but you're saving the future of our pack, and we could not be more grateful. We know that you will come to love it here just as we do."

I shake my head, tears threatening to spill through. "Reluctant? I was forced from the only piece of my father I've been given in thirteen years. That's all I had left. And now I have nothing."

The look on Sage's face as I gently pull my hands away almost leaves me regretful. "I'd like to be alone for a little bit, if that's okay."

Sage and Bailey share a look, then nod at me, leaving the room before shutting the door behind them. I don't mean to be cruel or immature in any way. But can they blame me for being upset? Sitting on the bed, I stare blankly out the window.

Elijah...I thought there could be possibly more with him. That we had a connection. But it was just some fucking mate bond. And then he rips me away from my home, my life...with no remorse.

Tears break free, streaming down my face.

I will never forgive him for this.

Chapter 12

Can We Please Stop Using the Term "Kidnap"

Elijah

Sighing, I pinch the bridge of my nose as I read the report from the warriors. More fucking rogue attacks. They had only gotten more frequent in the week since I brought Lucy here. Though I do regret the way things played out, it was for the best. She would have been dead in a day if I hadn't. And every day she's been here I'm constantly reminded of what happened between us, and how much she can't stand me.

A knock on the door brings me out of my thoughts. "Yes?" I call out, and Riftan cracks the door open stepping inside.

"What's up, Rif?" I ask, placing my pen down as I lean back in my chair. The last few times he's come in here it hasn't been good news, and right now I don't know how much more bad news I can take.

Sitting down in the chair across from me, he leans forward, resting his elbows on his thighs. "I have an update on Lucy."

Lucy. Just the sound of her name has my attention.

"I'm ready," I say, sitting up straight.

"She's still not leaving her room except for meal times." He grimaces. "In the beginning, it did seem like she was trying, but nobody approached her, so she just...retreated."

Fuck. Maybe giving the pack that warning had been a bad idea. How is she supposed to grow to love pack life if she never experiences pack life? I expected her anger at me. Hell, she hasn't even answered the door for me whenever I go to tell her "good morning" and "good night"...but to completely cut off everyone? I shake my head. "I've got to do something..." I mutter, mostly to myself.

My wolf has been restless since returning, constantly urging me to go see her, and more importantly, complete the mating bond. It's taken everything in my power not to march into her room, bend her over her bed, and—

"If I may?" Riftan asks, suddenly formal with me. He does this whenever he thinks I won't like what he's about to say.

"What is it?" I sigh, shaken from my thoughts of Lucy.

"I just..." He looks away nervously. "I don't know if she's going to adjust. It's been a week and she's still locked in her room. Maybe humans aren't cut out to be Luna—"

A sharp growl from my chest cuts off his train of thought. "Are you insinuating," I stand, walking around the desk, "that my Goddess-chosen, perfect match is not cut out to be Luna?"

"No, I just—"

"Because if you are," I continue, my wolf growling in my chest, "you're insinuating that I'm not 'cut out' to be Alpha."

He bows his head in submission. "Of course not. Forgive me, Alpha."

Placing a hand on his shoulder, I quietly admit, "while she is having a hard time now, I have seen her tenacity, and her commitment to the things she's passionate about."

Checking my watch, I pat him on the shoulder, his eyes meeting mine as he nods and I turn to leave the room. "Have you seen my sister?" I ask from over my shoulder.

"She was training with the other warriors when I passed by."

Nodding, I head down the stairs of the house, past the floor where the unmated warriors sleep, down through the kitchen, and out the back door. It's a brisk walk to the clearing where the warriors train, and they are just wrapping up for the day. As I approach, the warriors stop what they're doing, bowing their heads in deference. I may not have the Alpha Aura to command the submission, but I still get it out of respect.

"Alpha?" Bailey questions, leading the end-of-day stretches.

"I'll wait until you're done." I nod, crossing my arms and observing the routine.

They cycle through six more stretches, and end with a fierce howl. Smiling at them, I shake each warrior's hand as they leave the clearing, until it's only my sister and me left.

"So, what's up, Eli?" she asks, dropping the formalities now that we're alone.

"It's Lucy." I clench my jaw. "She doesn't leave her room except for meals, and even then, she doesn't talk to anyone."

She shrugs, using a towel to wipe the sweat off her brow. "You did kind of kidnap her. Did you really think that she would just immediately adjust to living with an entirely different species?"

Can we please stop using the term "kidnap"?

Irritation grows in my chest. "I didn't *kidnap* her, I was saving her life, I—" Letting out an exasperated breath, I shake my head. "It doesn't matter. I obviously didn't think she would just wake up and be acclimated. I just...I don't know. I guess I thought she would stop sulking and *try*."

"Uh-uh." Bailey shakes her head at me, pushing her finger into my chest. "Don't you dare say she's sulking. You go through everything she went through and tell me if you 'sulk' or not."

Fuck, she has a point.

At my silence, she sighs. "Have you tried asking her what's going on? How you can help?"

"She won't answer the door for me," I painfully admit.

"When was the last time you tried?" She raises a brow.

"Well I say goodnight and good morning, every single day..."

Bailey rolls her eyes so far I'd be surprised if she didn't see her brain. "That's not what I meant, Eli," she says softly, grabbing my arm. "When was the last time you knocked and said 'Lucy, can I come in?' or 'Lucy, will you talk to me?' or even 'Lucy, are you okay?'"

Gulping I avoid her eyes. Fuck, she's right. "I haven't."

"For all she knows, you're just saying your meaningless words and then walking away."

"I thought..." Rubbing the back of my neck, I look at the sky, as if searching for answers, "I thought she would just say something."

Bailey shakes her head. "She was removed from a familiar place, she has no friends, nobody to be close to her. I would, but I have Gamma duties." She shrugs. "As much as she denies it, you guys did connect...on a different level from the mate bond. A human level. Maybe she just needs you to talk to her."

Bailey chuckles as I whip around, and take off running back to the pack house. My feet pound up the steps, causing the warriors I pass to jump out of my way. I round the corner for the last flight of stairs to the top of the house—mine and Lucy's. Striding past my room and office, I make it to the end of the hall, gently rapping on the door. "Lucy..." My words catch in my throat. "C-can we talk?"

My keen hearing picks up movement on the other side of the door. A bed creaking slightly...footsteps padding toward the door. I step back as the door creaks open, her face peering up at me.

Goddess, she's even more beautiful than I remember. I haven't seen her face in a week, and I drink her in like a man dying of thirst. Her plump, pouty lips are turned down at me, her vibrant, green eyes in a scowl, her bouncy, golden brown hair is let loose around her face. Even pissed at me she's gorgeous.

"I'm not supposed to talk to strangers," she deadpans, but keeps the door cracked.

Wincing, I lean against the doorframe. "I guess I deserve that. Can I come in?"

"Fine," she concedes, taking a step back, opening the door further.

"Thank you." I step inside the room, taking a look at what she's done with the place.

Her notebook is on the bed, open, with a pen lying next to it and there's a stack of DVDs next to the TV. "I see you found the video library downstairs," I observe.

"You're about five years behind on all the good movies," she comments, picking at a nail.

"Yeah, well, we're slow to get things out here. Remember?" I pick up one of the DVDs. A cheesy rom-com. "I didn't peg you for the rom-com type." It's all I can do to keep myself from launching at her, my wolf is *not* happy that she hasn't been claimed yet. But I stand my ground. Things between Lucy and I are hard enough already, throwing myself at her and claiming her would be the last straw.

"Goes to show how little you actually know me," she replies with a sigh. "Is there a reason you came here other than to criticize my movie preferences?"

"Yeah..." Searching for words, I put the movie back on the stack. This shouldn't be so hard. She's my fated mate, but I've been fucking it all up. I push the words out anyway. "I wanted to talk to you...see how you're adjusting to life in the pack."

She actually snorts at me. "You would know if you actually came to see me once in the last week."

"That's why—"

Her eyes turn glassy as tears threaten to spill over. "You dragged me all the way out here, and then you left me alone, with no one to talk to! You uprooted my life, and then never even came to talk to me except for saying good morning and goodnight."

I can't help the indignation that grows in my chest. " If it weren't for me, those rogues would have killed you. I have been dealing with rogue attacks on my borders nonstop since last week, you aren't even *trying* to make friends here!"

She throws her arms into the air. "Why should I have to try? I'm not the one who dragged me here! You're selfish, and self-centered, and can't see beyond your pack!"

"I am responsible for this pack, Lucy! Their lives depend on how well I do my job, and they are some of the most selfless, kind, generous people you could ever meet! If you just gave them a chance—"

"Me? Give them a chance?" Lucy's voice breaks. "Your precious pack is so close minded that they won't even look in my direction, let alone speak to me. I have never been more lonely in my entire life, and I'm surrounded by people."

Her words break me. This is my fault. "Lucy, I..." Closing my eyes, I take a deep breath. "That may have been my fault."

"What?" Her voice, no longer on the verge of tears, makes me open my eyes.

"I...when we got here, I did a pack-wide mindlink. I could tell you were apprehensive about people accepting you because you're human, so I told them that if they so much as look at you wrong, there would be consequences. It seems that they may have taken that literally. I'll send out an amendment."

A laugh of disbelief escapes her, and she covers her mouth. "You said that?"

Feeling a smile grow on my face, I nod. "I did."

"Are werewolves normally such literal creatures?"

"We're wolf shifters, and not usually." I grimace. "But on the word of an Alpha..." Shrugging, I cross my arms. "Anything else on your mind?"

"You said I was just a human." She mirrors my stance, crossing her arms as well.

"You *are* a human," I remind her, "and you called me a dickhead, asshole, and a 'rude, brutish, inconsiderate fuck'."

"You kidnapped me," she counters, taking a step toward me.

"I saved your life," I correct, taking a step of my own.

"You destroyed my father's cabin." She closes the gap between us, uncrossing her arms.

"And then I fixed it," I breathe, my arms at my side now.

"You..." Her eyes dart down to my lips and I scent her growing arousal. Now that we've gotten everything out in the open, the tension between us is thick enough to cut it with a knife. I capture her mouth with mine, swallowing her words, as she throws her arms around my neck, deepening the kiss. Our lips move together, devouring each other with need. My tongue swipes her bottom lip, seeking entrance, and she lets me in, our tongues dancing and twining together. My wolf calms at *finally* having her again.

She withdraws so suddenly that I chase her lips. "I'm still mad at you." Her chest heaves with panting breaths.

"I know." I nod vigorously, my blood pumping so hard I can feel it in my ears. She can be mad at me forever as long as she keeps kissing me. Jumping into my arms, our mouths crashing yet again.

I drop her onto the bed, separating just for a moment so that I can take off her pants. A growl rumbles in my chest as I push two fingers between her folds. "So wet for me," I murmur, gliding my fingers around, spreading her wetness all over. She throws her head back and whimpers. My thumb rubs over her clit as my fingers pump in and out of her, causing her whimpers to grow to moans, which capture my mouth in an all consuming kiss.

My length strains against my pants and twitches when she scrambles at my belt. Withdrawing my fingers, I stand on my knees, undoing my belt, before shimmy off my pants and underwear, while she removes her last layer separating us. Caging myself over her, I use one hand to guide myself towards her entrance, sucking in a breath as I enter her, her deep moan encouraging me to enter all the way to the hilt.

"Fuck, Elijah," she gasps, her nails digging into my shoulder, the sting feeding into my arousal as I withdraw and enter her again full force. Her cries grow louder as I pound into her, her legs wrapping tight around my waist. I'm going harder than I mean to, but it only seems to deepen her arousal. She bucks her hips in time with mine, pushing me deeper than ever. I reach one hand between us, stroking her clit in time with my thrusts, her cries reaching a peak, as her walls contract around my cock when she comes.

Slowing my thrusting in time with hers, she lets her legs fall from my back, a satiated sigh escaping her lips. "Done already?" I ask, pressing a slow kiss to her neck, gently nipping at her before looking at her face. My wolf whines at me, my lips so close to the actual spot of claiming, where all I would have to do is bite right where her neck meets her shoulder…

She's not ready for that yet.

"Not a chance," she challenges, pushing me off of her, and onto my back. Her legs straddle me as she slowly lowers herself onto my cock, sinking all the way down until our bodies are flush again.

Riding me, she braces her hands on my chest, and I revel at the sight above me. Her glorious body on full display—her round, perky tits, the feel of her perfect ass in my hands as she bounces up and down on me, and her face…fuck. I could get used to seeing that look of ecstasy on her beautiful face.

I'm getting close, but before I come, she shudders again, her breaths erratic, and she meets my eyes, her chest heaving. I'm a goner.

Flipping us around so she's on her knees, I drive into her relentlessly, the slapping of her thighs hitting mine the only other sound besides our breathing, her moans of pleasure. I'm so fucking close to the edge, my cock swells as my knot begins to form. I pulled out last time, ensuring she didn't have to feel it, but that was before she knew I was a wolf. I slam into her full force as she cries out, and I tumble over the edge, my orgasm spilling into her.

The knot secures us in place. Though she doesn't seem to notice.

"Oh, Lucy..." I bend over, resting my head on her back as we fall into bed together, a tangled heap of limbs, lust, and sweat. My cock still nestled inside her. As happy as I am, I can't say my wolf is entirely pleased. His disgruntled howls an echo of his protest that once again, I've not allowed him to claim her.

Not like he wants.

Chapter 13

As You Command, Alpha

Lucy

My eyes crack open as the light from the balcony doors hits my face. My body is sore, but in a deliciously good way. Stretching my arms over my head, I roll onto my side to see if Elijah stayed the night or left after I fell asleep. I'm not sure what I'm hoping for, or what last night even meant for that matter, but I do know that was some damn good sex.

My heart sinks slightly when I see his side of the bed is empty, but then I notice the note on his pillow, still indented from where his head was resting.

"*Lucy,*

You looked too gorgeous to wake—I have some pack things to take care of. I've let the pack know I was too harsh in my earlier statement, so the whole avoiding you thing should stop. Now that they have the courage to speak to you, I'm sure they will be just as smitten with you as I am.

Don't worry about the rogue attacks, as long as you stay close to the homes on the pack grounds, you'll be safe.

I'm sorry for not realizing how alone you were all this time, and

I plan on rectifying that immediately. If you want, I'd like it if you met me by the frozen pond at 11.

-Elijah"

Below the note, he had scribbled a hand-drawn map of where to go. I feel my cheeks lift in a grin, but quickly try to stifle it. No, he didn't get out of it that easily. He brought me here against my will. But, I have been thinking about it, and I probably would have regretted staying. I don't want to think about what would have happened if the rogue wolves came back, and I can't expect Elijah to stay at the cabin to take care of me forever.

But that was my choice to make!

Would it be worth making my own choice if it was one that got me killed? Probably not.

But it's beside the point. I should have had the choice to figure it out myself. And as much as I want to stay mad at him...it doesn't help that he's saying all the right things...

Not to mention doing *all the right things...*

My cheeks heat at the memory of his hand between my legs, and the way he looked at me while I was riding him. The thoughts send a shiver down my spine that have me kicking my feet like some sort of lovestruck teenager. Shit, I don't think anyone in the world has sex as amazing as this. If they did, nobody would ever do anything else. Ever.

The only reason why I'm not hunting him down for round two right now is because I'm still kind of pissed at him for bringing me here. Though...I mean...I *do* feel safer here. There's no wolves staring at me through my window, which is ironic considering I'm now actually living among werewolves.

Picking up the note again, I reread the hastily scribbled words, and the way he drew a little house to represent the house where he lives. It's kind of cute. Grinning, and trying to ignore my now pounding heart, I get up, pulling on some warm clothes courtesy of the walk-in closet, and venture out of the house.

The change among the members of the pack is staggering. Now, instead of hastily looking away, or outright changing directions when they see me, many smile and nod, others actually stop and greet me as *Luna*, which I admit, kind of freaks me out. As soon as I say, "Oh, please, call me Lucy," their smiles light up and they thank me for coming to the pack. Looking around, I wonder where Bailey is. I feel bad for ignoring her when she tried to talk to me that first day, maybe I should seek her out after this.

So far, it doesn't seem like anyone has an issue with me being human, but I still keep my eyes open, just in case.

I'm focusing on the little map in my hand, looking up just as I reach the small decline that leads to the frozen pond. It takes me less than a second to spot Elijah, standing next to a bench that faces the pond, holding up two pairs of ice skates, grinning like a madman.

I try to keep the smile off my face, but I know that at least one corner of my mouth tugs up because his eyes crinkle in an annoyingly adorable way as he waves me down the hill to join him. My boots crunch in the snow as I shuffle down the hill, and when I reach him, there's a hint of amusement in my voice. "Ice skating?"

"I just thought..." I swear his cheeks turn a little red. "It's something we can do outside, together, with little chance of us stopping to have sex before we actually have a conversation."

"Do you object to having sex with me?" I tease.

He rolls his eyes. "Of course not, but since you are so skeptical about the mate bond, I figured we could do this, you know, the *human* way."

"This?"

"You know...dating?"

That is...

So fucking thoughtful.

I fight the smirk that's fighting its way onto my mouth. "You want to *date* me?"

He rolls his eyes, pushing the skates into my hands, "Just put on the fucking ice skates."

"As you command, *Alpha*." I laugh, sitting on the bench.

"Don't do that." His voice is strained, and his eyes…they're flicking back and forth between blue and black.

"Do…what?" I'm entranced by the way his eyes are reacting to me, and I wonder just what kind of effect I have on him.

"Don't…uh…don't submit to me."

"I was just kidding—"

"I know, but my wolf doesn't understand sarcasm, and when you do that, he urges me to…"

"To what?" My voice is barely a whisper.

"To *claim* you." His voice wavers slightly, and I swallow, nodding tightly.

Breaking the tension, I take a seat on the bench to lace up my skates, Elijah following suit. "Your wolf?" I feel like I should ask Elijah for a werewolf dictionary with all the new words and phrases I'm learning.

"What about it?"

"Well, I don't know, I guess I just had it in my head that you turn into a wolf, but that it's still…well…you. I didn't think there was anyone else hanging out," I point to his head, "in there. And claiming? What is that? Is it different from sex?"

"Hm." He finishes lacing up his skates thoughtfully. "I've never really thought of it before. It's like, right now, he's here, but kind of in the backseat. And then, when I'm in wolf form, his instincts drive all my survival actions, but I'm driving the conscious thoughts. Does that make sense?"

It does, to an extent. I'm not sure I'll ever fully understand it though, not without experiencing it for myself. The next words are out of my mouth before I know what I'm saying, "Can I… meet him? Sometime?"

"He'd like that." He grins at me, helping me to my feet. "And as for the claiming...it's the final step to complete the mate bond. Sex is typically a precursor but not required, but it ends with me biting you," he drags a finger to the spot where my neck meets my shoulder, sending a shiver through me, "right here."

Woah. I can see why sex is a precursor.

Needing a cool down, I turn away. "Um, Elijah?" Holding his hand, I decide to change the subject, wobbling toward the pond.

"What's wrong?" His brow furrows as he looks at me.

Looking up sheepishly at him, I admit, "I don't know how to ice skate."

An actual laugh erupts from his chest. "Aren't you from Rhode Island?"

"Hey, my grandparents were too old to take me when I moved out there with them." I find myself laughing with him.

"That's okay." He smiles at me, and my heart flutters. "I'll teach you."

We step onto the ice, and he skates a few circles while I try to get my feet situated. Immediately, my feet start moving apart from each other, almost forcing me to do the splits.

"Uh, Elijah!" I call out, panicking, and he quickly skates back over to me, hoisting me up by my elbows.

"You have to keep your feet perpendicular to your body," he says, "So they don't spread out like that."

"I know *that*."

"If you know that, then why aren't you doing it?"

"Because doing it is the hard part!" I nearly scream as I grip his arms for dear life.

"Here." He moves so that he is facing me, and then slowly moves his feet so he's skating backwards while holding my hands. "Match my foot movements. Keep your feet straight. If you feel your feet getting away from you again, just use me as leverage and fix your footing."

Nodding, I concentrate on his feet, watching his movements and trying to mirror them. I feel like I might have it for a moment, but somehow, I end up falling forward, knocking him backwards onto the ice, and landing on top of him. "Oof," he lets out, patting my back. "Are you okay?"

"I'm so sorry!" I scramble to try to stand up, but somehow that just makes it worse and I land backwards on my ass.

He stands, reaching out a hand to help me up. Taking it, I grimace as I stand, worried that he is already regretting bringing me on this date.

"So..." he says, dusting the ice off of my back. "You really can't skate, huh?"

Something between us breaks and we both dissolve into laughter. "I fucking told you!" I laughed, struggling so hard to stay upright that Elijah comes to my side and loops my arm through his.

"I don't know, I thought maybe you were one of those falsely modest people who claim they don't know how to skate but are actually like a professional level ice skater." This has us doubling over laughing even more, and he guides us off the pond, where we collapse onto the bench in a fit of giggles.

We are just changing out of our ice skates and into our shoes when a figure comes over the hill. "I thought I heard some laughing over here."

My jaw almost drops at the woman who traipses down the hill like she owns the place. Long, straight blonde hair, blue eyes, tan skin, and athletic build...she looked like she could be on the cover of a sports illustrated magazine.

I can't help but notice that physically, she's the exact opposite of me.

"Hi there. Elijah," she croons, giving him doe eyes. My jaw almost drops as she turns to me. "I've heard so much about you, Kelly, right? I'm Thallia."

"Lucy," I correct, gritting my teeth. So she was one of *those* kinds of girls.

"Lucy." She gives a fake smile. "And just look at your hair. Those waves would look unruly and messy on anyone else, but you...they look right at home on you."

Did she just...? Fuck no.

Before I can ask her what the fuck her problem is, Elijah asks her, "so how was your trip? Was New York everything you thought it would be?"

"And then some." She flashes her teeth. "Though, it would have been even better with the company of a certain Alpha with me."

This time, my jaw *does* drop.

What the fuck is going on here?

My eyes flit between Thallia and Elijah as he laughs. He fucking *laughs*. "You know I'm not built for those kinds of crowds." He turns to me. "Thallia and I grew up together in the pack. She's practically my second sister," he says, as if that explains why she is looking at him like he's a piece of steak she wants to eat for dinner.

She reaches over to touch his bicep, and does this fucking ridiculous pouty thing with her lips. "I don't know, Elijah, I'd say we're *much* closer than typical siblings." I want to wrench her fucking hand off of his arm and ask what kind of incestuous shit she's into if she thinks this is normal sibling behavior, but instead, I smile tightly as she bats her eyes at him, him seemingly unaware of her ulterior motives.

Elijah grins at me like he's so glad she came over and introduced herself, but honestly, is he that fucking dense? Because he's saying she's like a sister to him, but Thallia acts as if she's gunning for a shotgun ride on the Elijah Express.

Chapter 14

Santa Claws

Lucy

Wiping the sweat from my brow, I observe my handiwork laid out on the kitchen island. It's been four days since Elijah and I made up, or well, since I'd forgiven him. Turns out he's pretty hard to stay mad at. After we got back from ice skating, I had wanted to bake the chocolate chip cookies Mom and I used to make to take my mind off of how Thallia had acted towards Elijah. A couple of batches were cooling when some of the warriors came back from training, asked if they could try one, and then before I knew it, they were devoured, only crumbs left in their wake.

You would think that I'd be upset, but surprisingly, I was... happy. Seeing their eyes light up or roll to the back of their head I should say, when they would bite into something I had made...it made me feel like I had become a step closer to my mom, and how she brought people joy with food. I could see that I brought joy to Elijah's pack, and it made me feel a little more welcome.

So I kept baking. I started cooking dinners, lunches, and breakfasts. Pack members started talking to me more. I found that when all else fails, food is the thing that can bring people together.

Family style dinners became a thing, all of us sitting around the large dining room table instead of people staggering in at all hours or taking food up to their rooms.

Elijah has been extremely busy with all the rogue activity, but he always makes it to meals...well, dinner anyway. Last night at dinner, Elijah squeezed my thigh as he sat next to me, a light in his eyes I couldn't quite place, but I knew it made my stomach feel like it was doing acrobatics. I wasn't sure when it had happened, but over the last few days, the cooking and baking had become less about feeling close to my mom, and more about feeling close to them.

The pack.

Don't think I'll ever get used to saying that with a straight face.

Laid out before me were some rice krispy treats, brookies, and salted caramel cookies. Gathering a bit of each into some ziploc bags, I grab a large tote and pile them in, careful not to smash anything.

I'd started hand delivering the goodies to the families with young children two days ago. The parents are grateful, but the real motivator is the kids. The way their little eyes light up when they see me coming with my basket of treats makes me feel like fucking Santa Claus.

Or Santa Claws.

Chuckling to myself, I stomp on my boots, bundling myself in my coat and jacket, my bag of goodies hanging from my elbow. I've delivered treats to all but the very last house on the outskirts of the pack territory. The sun is starting to go down, and it's uncharacteristically quiet. I get the distinct feeling that someone... or some*thing* is watching me.

I'm suddenly feeling a lot less like Santa Claus, and a whole lot more like Little Red Riding Hood being watched by the Big Bad Wolf. Swallowing and shaking my head, I continue towards the last house. Elijah said as long as I stayed within pack territory, I'm safe. The sound of a branch snapping has me whipping my head around to face...Thallia?

"Kelly," she greets me, her head tilting slightly.

"Tapioca," I level, praying that my body doesn't betray me and show her just how terrified I am to be out here alone.

"It's Thallia." She scowls for a moment, then her face relaxes. "Honest mistake. What are you doing out here?"

"Oh..." My cheeks flush as I lift my tote of goodies in explanation. "Treat delivery. I only have one left." I gesture further down the treeline to the last house on the territory.

"Ah, the Meyers. Silvy will love those." Her tone is pleasant, she sounds almost fond of the youngest child in the Meyers family. Could she actually be a decent person and we just got off on the wrong foot?

"Yeah, she asked for more Rice Krispy Treats." I found myself smiling.

"Care if I walk with you?" she asks cordially, and I nod, continuing my walk through the snow.

We trudge in silence for a moment before Thallia speaks. "You know, I'm so relieved that Elijah finally found his mate. He's been searching for years."

"You seem to care a great deal about him," I observe, trying to give her the benefit of the doubt.

"Oh, I care more than you could ever know." She slides her eyes over me before continuing, "it broke my heart every time he would sleep with one of the females in the pack, trying to get a mate bond to snap into place. He was so desperate at one point he was taking two at a time. I was getting really worried about him."

My heart stutters at her words. Elijah...sleeping around? He said he didn't do the one night stand thing. That if he slept with me, I was his. Just how many were there? Trying not to let her words affect me, I try to keep my voice level as I answer her, "well, as you said, he's found his mate now."

"That's the thing." She taps a finger to her chin thoughtfully. "I wonder if you really are his mate. I mean, no offense, Kelly—"

"Lucy," I grit out, not liking the turn this conversation was taking.

"Lucy." She gives me a fake ass smile. "It just seems so convenient that he would have a mate that can't actually feel the mate bond. All you have to go on is his word alone."

But I did feel *something*...didn't I?

"That's not—" I'm not sure if I'm trying to defend him or myself, but in either case, I'm cut off.

"Oh, well." She waves her hand dismissively. "Mate or not, I'm sure he'll get bored of you eventually since you're just a human and don't have the *bite* that males need to fulfill their desires." She keeps her face as innocent as possible. "Best you just run off now before feelings run too deep."

Clenching my fists, I take a deep breath, trying to keep from launching myself at this bitch.

My voice comes out a growl, "You don't know—"

"Oh, Lucy, don't be mad. I'm just looking out for you. I know what's going to happen, and I'm trying to warn you. I don't understand why you would willingly walk into that."

We've reached the house at the edge of the territory. Without a word, I ring the doorbell, drop the last of the treats on their doorstep, and take off in the opposite direction, away from Thallia even as I feel her gaze burrow into my back. One step in front of the other towards the pack house.

My house.

My boots crunch in the snow, my feet carrying me as fast as they can back to my refuge. My mate. Thallia isn't right. I know I feel something on my side of the mate bond. But my heart lurches at the fact that she might be right about one thing. What if I don't have the *bite*?

My heart sinks into my stomach at the thought that I might lose Elijah right when I was starting to get used to being in this place.

Since he cleared things up with the pack, they were doing more to make me feel welcome. And he was right, there are a lot of amazing people here. To think that could all be so quickly taken away, slightly breaks my heart.

A knock on my door shifts my focus from the rom-com playing on TV. I wait for someone to speak on the other side, as they usually do whenever someone comes knocking, but there's no sound.

Hm.

Opening my door, I peek out quickly only to be met with an empty hall. Glancing down, I see an envelope on the floor, next to what looks like a string bikini. Frowning, I grab it, thumbing through the contents. A typed note, and a small, hand drawn map.

Dear Lucy,

I've been wanting to show you the hot springs around here. A delicious treat for sore muscles, among other things. Please meet me as soon as possible. I've included a map for you, and a bathing suit to wear. Your clothes will stay dry if you leave them on the twin rocks that back the hot spring.

-Elijah

The tone of the note was different than I was used to...a little more formal compared to his last letter he left me. Maybe he didn't have time to sit and hand write it this time. Frowning, I find the map that he drew for me for our ice skating date...the penmanship of the map looks pretty similar. Grinning, I shut the door and pull on my bathing suit, ready to melt the stress away with the man I'm starting to care so deeply for.

Walking through the snow at night with a bikini under my clothes is not something that I thought I would check off my bucket list, but here we are. I follow the directions until I reach the twin rocks that back the hot spring as indicated by the map. I don't see Elijah anywhere, but there's nothing wrong with getting a head start. Maybe I'll give him a little surprise of my own. Grinning, I strip off everything but my boots and swimsuit, shivering as I practically run to the hot spring.

Frowning as I get closer, I come to the other side of the rocks and...what the hell? The water is frozen. Just like the pond Elijah and I were ice skating on. I check the map again, thinking I made a wrong turn somewhere. Turning to grab my clothes, my mouth gapes open when I see that they aren't on the rock where I left them.

My gut turns...someone set me up. What the fuck. It feels like I've had the rug ripped out from under me, all feelings of belonging stripped from me, leaving me as emotionally bare as my body. Goosebumps trail up my skin, cooling my anger for now. I'd figure out who did this, and they would pay. But for now, I need to make my way back to the pack house without freezing to death. Wrapping my arms around me, I trek through the snow back towards the pack house. Did Elijah do this?

No.

He wouldn't have done this. He cares about me. It could have been Thallia or any of the other werewolves who wouldn't even look at me until a couple of days ago. Maybe I didn't fit in as well as I thought I did because of a few cookies. As I contemplate the possibilities, a voice calls for me.

"Lucy! Lucy, where are you, baby?"

"I'm here!" I choke out, my teeth chattering. Thank god or the Moon Goddess or whoever the fuck I need to thank for werewolf hearing.

"Oh, Lucy." His face falls when he sees me, and he immediately takes off his jacket to wrap around me, lifting me tenderly in his arms, and starts walking back in the direction of the pack house.

"How did you know where I was?" I ask quietly, burrowing my head against his chest, greedily gathering his warmth.

"I went to your room, but you weren't there. I found a note on the bed and realized what happened. I'm so sorry, Lucy. I left immediately to find you."

I know he's trying to make me feel better, but all I feel is stupid. "I'm sorry." A tear slides down my cheek. "It must be so embarrassing to have a stupid human for a mate."

A growl erupts from his chest, and he uses a hand to cup my face. "Never. Never apologize for being human. You are *not* an embarrassment. The only embarrassment here is whoever decided to pull a stunt like this—whoever *dared* to put my future Luna in danger."

My heart skips a beat.

Not *a* Luna.

Not *the* Luna.

His Luna.

Maybe Thallia doesn't know what she's talking about afterall. Swallowing roughly, I lean into his touch. He sighs. "I will find out who did this. I swear it to you, Lucy."

He sets me down gently, and I realize that we are in front of the secondary pack house—we live in the primary pack house. This one has all three floors housing unmated wolves. He places the gentlest of kisses on my lips, and murmurs to me. "I am going to look and sound very scary in there. I'm keeping my rage in check for your sake, Lu, but what you see and hear...it's who I am. I'm the Alpha." He lifts my chin to look me in the eyes. "And you are their future Luna. They must respect us both or they have no place in this pack."

Nodding, I watch as he bursts through the front door, his voice booming. "Who would dare hurt my mate? Your future Luna!"

Swallowing, I peek inside, noting the way the other werewolves bow their heads in submission. Only Riftan comes up to him. "What happened?"

Elijah peeks back at me, rage swimming in his eyes, before he turns to address the room. "Someone impersonated me by leaving a letter for Lucy. I will not divulge the details, but whoever did this is lucky I was there to find her. You will help me find who did this, or so help me..."

One of the warriors speaks up. "Yes, Alpha. We will do everything in our power. I think I speak for everyone here when I say that we will be beyond blessed by the Moon Goddess to have Lucy as our Luna, and we will not stand for her being harmed."

Murmurs of agreement spread through the room, and my cheeks warm in gratitude. Here I thought one of them might be the one who set me up, but based on their words now...and Elijah? The way he stormed in there to come to my defense? Damn, that was hot.

I was so lost in thought I didn't realize Elijah had come back out of the house until he had swooped me back into his arms, carrying back toward the pack house.

I hiss as Elijah lowers me into the clawed bathtub, my teeth still chattering from being out in the cold. "Shhhh, it's okay, baby, I've got you," he murmurs softly to me as he moves behind the tub and grabs one of my arms, dunking it beneath the surface before massaging it under the water.

A groan escapes my lips as he moves his hands up to my shoulders, his expert fingers kneading my sensitive flesh, the trills of excitement from the mate bond only adding to the experience. His hands move deftly across my shoulders, and finding my other arm, he peppers kisses on my neck. "Nobody will ever do anything like that to you again," he whispers between kisses, his hands moving back along my arm to my shoulders again.

"Do you promise?" I ask quietly, my eyes closed, reveling in the way his hands move across my skin.

"I suppose I can't promise they won't try." He nips my earlobe, causing me to gasp. "But I *can* promise that when I find who did this, and I swear to the Moon Goddess that *I will find them*," he nibbles down my neck, "I will make such an example of them that anyone who dares think such treacherous thoughts about my mate would rather burn themselves alive than cross me."

A sigh leaves my throat as his hands leave my shoulders, falling to cup my breasts. "What will you do to them? You won't kill them...will you?"

"Oh no, much worse than that." I can feel his smile against my neck as he kneads my flesh, causing heat to pool in my center. "I'll strip them of their tie to the pack. They'll be kicked out of the pack lands and no longer a part of our family. Some say it's a fate worse than death."

"You would do that for me?" I gasp as his hands splay down my stomach, entering the water.

"Lucy, there is nothing I wouldn't do for you...to you." There's an edge to his voice as his hands drift lower, slipping into my folds. A shuddering gasp leaves my mouth as he rubs circles around my clit, my back arching up against the back of the tub.

"Fuck, Elijah!" I cry out, writhing under his expert touch before his free hand draws under my chin, pulling my mouth to his. He swallows my cries as his fingers in my core bring me higher and higher, so close to the edge. He takes my bottom lip gently between his teeth and pulls, sending me over and into oblivion.

My hips buck under his hands as my orgasm rides itself out, my movement slowing as I come down completely.

"Elijah." My voice is thick.

"What is it, baby?" His eyes are closed, his forehead against mine.

"I think I'm warmed up."

His eyes shoot open, and he grabs me out of the bath, not even bothering with a towel before he hauls me over his shoulder out of my bathroom, placing me on the bed.

He strips off his clothes, holding himself over me, kissing me deeply, moving down my neck, pulling one of my nipples into his mouth—

"Eli," I gasp, and he pauses, "I want to touch you—"

Dropping my nipple, he comes up to my face. "Not tonight, baby."

My brow furrows. "Why?"

"I could have lost you. If I didn't come up here and see that letter, who knows what could have happened. You could have gotten lost and froze to death." His voice chokes up, "You could have wandered past pack territory—"

"Hey, hey, hey," I cut him off, grabbing his face in my hands. "I'm here. You did find me." I kiss him deeply, and pull back to look at his face again, his blue eyes piercing into mine. "You *did* find me. I'm safe."

"I know." His voice trembles. "I haven't been to see you as much as I should have, Lu. I let this happen to you. If I wasn't so caught up with all the rogue attacks…I'm sorry. I want to show you how much you mean to me."

I nod. "Okay, Eli. It's okay." He kisses me deeper, more slowly than he was before. He moves down to my breasts, paying each one special attention, his hot mouth enveloping all of the sensitive flesh, while his fingers circle my clit again.

A moan escapes me as he moves down to kiss my stomach, placing a deep, sensual kiss on each of my hip bones before finally, blissfully, running his tongue up my center. A sharp cry leaves me at the sudden increase of pleasure, but he doesn't let up. His hands grasp the insides of my thighs and hold them open while he devours me, licking and nipping and sucking in ways that have me bucking my hips against his face, my hands in his hair.

He growls in approval, the vibration sending out another cry from me. Before he inserts a finger, pumping it in and out in time with his tongue's movements, until I finally tumble over the edge of bliss, his name on lips as I unravel.

I lay on the bed, a satiated, limp mess. As he crawls up next to me, tucking my body into his, no part of our bodies not touching. To say I'm wary of this place now, would be an understatement. Part of me wants to tell him what I think—or at least who I think wrote that letter, but I don't.

The last thing I want to do is start issues where there aren't any. Even if Thallia's comments still rattle through my mind on a never ending loop.

Chapter 15

Fucking Thallia

Lucy

I can't sleep.

I've been laying in this bed for hours and still my body wants nothing more than to obsess over Thallia and what her intentions are with Elijah. Last night when Eli brought me back to this room and took care of me...bathing me, massaging me, then burrowing his head between my legs, it was the sweetest I'd ever seen him. He obviously cares about me. In fact, I had to bar him from sleeping with me tonight because I knew if he did, we'd have sex at some point, and I was trying to get a good night's sleep.

So why can't I get fucking Thallia out of my head? I twist and turn, trying to get comfortable as my brain plays over all of Thallia's words about what he did while he was trying to find his mate. Was that the only reason he slept with me? No, I know that's not true.

This morning, when I woke up with my back snug against his body with his arm securely around my waist, I had wiggled out of his grasp enough that I turned around and kissed him. That kiss led to the laziest, sweetest, most satisfying morning fuck I've ever had. Laying on his chest after, I asked him when he realized he was my mate. He said it was when I handed him the oatmeal on our first morning together at my cabin. He had seemed interested in me even before that, especially considering our conversation about our dads in the living room, and the way he spoke to me in the kitchen while I was cooking.

I can't shake the jealousy of imagining him with so many other women. It's not like I don't have a history, but I'm not living as a family unit with Horny Professor. Then again, if Elijah said that he knew when he touched me, why would he need to *sleep* with all those women? I want to stuff my face into my pillow and scream. I should just ask him. I should get over myself and ask him if it's true that he's slept with nearly every woman in the pack.

But he has enough on his plate without having to deal with my insecure ass.

Fucking Thallia. She had to be messing with me. Sighing, I replay their interaction by the pond in my mind, remembering how Elijah acted. He didn't reach out and touch her. Hell, he didn't even look at her any different than he would look at Bailey.

Hm. Maybe I should ask Bailey if she knows anything about them. Do they have a history, or is Thallia really straight forward? I know that no matter what the answer is I won't like it, because either Thallia has big balls to blatantly act like that with his mate right there, or there's some sort of romantic history that he hasn't told me about.

My boots crunch in the snow as I take a walk the next morning. I'm tired, frustrated, and my insecurity is nearly eating me alive. I'm sure I look like a complete mess this morning, my hair pulled into a messy braid, my beanie over my head and a huge coat swallowing me. I think I finally got to sleep around three in the morning, but it was one of those restless sleeps where you wake up and aren't sure if you slept at all.

Before long, I'm at the top of the hill that overlooks the pond that Elijah and I skated on nearly a week ago. Despite my grouchiness, I smile at the memory of that day, and I wonder what we had looked like from here, falling over each other, laughing hysterically.

"Penny for your thoughts?" a voice startles me out of my thoughts, making me jump, wiping the smile off my face.

Fucking Thallia.

Her Barbie-like appearance is only accentuated by her hair pulled up into a high ponytail, her hot pink sweater showing off her incredible figure. All she needs is pink sunglasses and a designer handbag, and she could be the prototype for Werewolf Barbie.

Damn, I hate her.

Unable to keep the aggravation out of my voice, I scowl at her. "What, are you like, following me or something?"

Her sickly sweet smile makes my stomach turn. "Not at all. I just happened to catch the scent of...human."

Grunting, I turn away from her, ready to make the trek back to the pack house. Of course, the bitch follows me. "I heard about the prank someone pulled on you yesterday." At my silence, she continues, "it's unfortunate that happened. The hard thing is it could have been anyone."

I stop, staring hard at her, anger churning in my gut. "What do you know?"

"Oh, nothing." Thallia smiles again. "I mean, we are wolves after all. Did you really think that baking treats and making dinner would make everyone forget that you're a human?" She chuckles and tilts her head at me. "I know that they act nice, but you need to be careful...enemies are everywhere."

I continue walking away and this time she stays where she is. "I'm just looking out for you!" she calls after me as tears sting my eyes.

Fucking. Thallia.

Enemies are everywhere? I know she just said that to get to me, but...what if she is right? What if one of the wolves that I'd been feeding and baking for hated me so much that they would put me in danger like that.

I need to talk to Elijah. We'll talk about what Thallia said, and he can clear up any misunderstandings. Easy peasy. I don't know why I didn't come to this conclusion sooner. Stomping through the back door of the pack house, I leave my boots on the rack in the back of the kitchen. I was already tired from barely sleeping last night, but now I'm in an even worse mood after talking to Thallia.

Shuffling up the stairs and into my room, I toss my heavy coat, hat, and gloves on my bed, leaving me in just my leggings and a sweater. Pulling on a fresh pair of thick, wooly socks, I pad down the hallway to Elijah's office.

"Elijah?" I knock on his office door.

"Come in," he calls, and I crack the door open to see him hunched over his desk, looking over paperwork. His black hair is pushed back, like he's been constantly running his fingers through his hair, and his blue eyes look tired, just like mine. His shirt is rumpled and the top two buttons are undone, giving me a peek of his tattoo on his chest. It's not like I haven't seen it before, but damn it's sexy peeking out at me like that. His sleeves are pushed up to his elbows, showing off his muscular forearms. "Lucy, baby, is everything okay?" he asks, his concerned eyes looking over me.

"Yes...I mean no—I don't know." Shaking my head, I sit in a chair on the other side of his desk. "I ran into Thallia, and she said some...some things."

"What kinds of things?" He asks, a frown forming on his lips.

"Just now, she said that the accident was unfortunate, and that I can't trust anyone because enemies are everywhere."

Elijah shrugs his shoulders, almost like he's brushing off my concern. "It sounds like she was just looking out for you, if not being a little paranoid."

Anger rolls in my gut. "No, Eli. You don't understand. The way that she said it...she *laughed* as she said it. Her tone...it wasn't concerned. It sounded like a warning."

Sighing, he leans back in his chair. "I'm sure you just misunderstood. Thallia is an odd one, but she means well. We're looking into who pulled that stunt the other day, and like I said, once I find them, they're out of the pack."

Swallowing, I nod. Elijah went back to whatever he was doing, and silently, I get up and head back to the door. Anger boils inside me like a pot threatening to roll over.

Why isn't he grasping what I'm telling him? Why isn't he taking my concern seriously? My hand grasps the doorknob, and I can't keep the venom from my voice. "Was she just looking out for me when she told me about the countless women you fucked in search of your mate?"

The rustling of papers stops, and I dare to turn my gaze towards him. His brows are furrowed, his mouth slightly open. I continue, almost choking on my words, "about how you got so desperate at one point that you were routinely bringing in *two at a time?*"

Shaking his head, he stands, and as he walks to me. "I mean, it's none of my business. It was before you met me, but fuck, Elijah, do I have to know about it? Look at every woman here and wonder which ones you've had your dick in—"

A growl escapes him before he reaches me, grabbing my face in his hands and kissing me fiercely. "That. Never. Happened."

"Why did she say it then?" I ask quietly, wrapping my hands around his wrists. I'm so frustrated, so angry at how helpless I feel and at this situation, that I don't even notice the tear that rolls down my cheek until Elijah catches it with his thumb.

"At one point..." He sighs, almost as if he were searching for words. "I called each woman into my office and I touched them."

At my gasp and attempt to pull away, he tightens his grip on me. "Not like that, Lucy. A touch to the arm. A handshake. I didn't tell anyone why, it was before anyone else knew that my father put in that fucking stipulation about me becoming Alpha. Rumors must have started going around..." He shook his head. "I messed around with some females when I was younger, before my father died. I was a teenager, and stupid. But you were the first since he died."

I swallow, my brain struggling to perform the most basic mental math at his confession. "You hadn't had sex in..."

"Three years." He nodded, "I'm serious about you, Lucy, and not just because you're my mate. Honestly, I'm lucky as fuck you ended up being my mate because even if you weren't, I would have fallen for you anyway."

My heart stutters at his confession, and I kiss him tenderly. Despite his words, there's still something nagging at me. Pulling back, I place a hand on his chest. "But why would Thallia say that to me unless she was trying to hurt me?"

Running a hand through his hair, he pulls me against his chest. "I'm sure she just genuinely believed the rumors and wanted to make sure you knew what you were getting into. I can't really blame her for that. I'll talk to her and set the record straight. She must really care for you if she was willing to risk my anger and tell you the rumors anyway."

My mouth gapes open as I lean my head against his chest. He doesn't see it. Why doesn't he see it? His blindness when it comes to her is infuriating. Taking a deep breath and controlling my voice, I tell him, "Thank you for listening, I'll let you get back to work now."

His chest rises and falls heavily. "Yeah, I suppose I should get back to it." He releases me, planting a kiss in my hair before he murmurs in my ear, "we'll continue this tonight," using a hand to squeeze my ass. Butterflies flip in my belly as he winks at me, going back to his desk.

Fine. I'll let the matter rest for now, but if I get any more feelings that she's even breathing funny, I'll bring it up again, and next time, I won't stop until he really hears me.

Chapter 16

Full Moon

Lucy

It's a full moon tonight.

Two weeks have passed since I confronted Elijah in his office about Thallia. It's the second full moon since I was brought here, but I missed the first one staying in my room and refusing to speak to anyone.

A group of warriors meet in front of the pack house, the sight of them all transforming into wolves has me entranced. Elijah wasn't lying about werewolves being pretty indifferent about nudity, because all the figures, whether they're male or female, are stark naked in the snow, illuminated by the light of the full moon. There's something beautiful—poetic even—about the way their bodies move as they shift from human to wolf.

Mesmerized by the sight, my breath fogs the window in front of me. I keep my eyes on the wolves as they disappear into the woods, running freely and howling into the night.

Anything I know about werewolves comes from scary movies and Halloween. The wolves I live with are anything but gruesome though. Graceful, majestic, and terrifying in a way, but not horrible like the movies depict them. It makes me question what else the movies have wrong. Does the full moon have any physical impact on them? Obviously they can shift whenever they want, so maybe it's a religious thing. Or they're stronger under the light of the full moon.

The sight of a figure further up the tree line catches my attention. The moonlight illuminates the figure, hunched over and wearing a hood as they walk towards the trees. A flash of blonde hair flies out of their hood and makes my blood freeze. They quickly turn their head, seemingly scanning their surroundings, and I glimpse their face.

Fucking Thallia.

What the hell is she doing? Why is she sneaking off into the woods in the middle of the night? Whirling towards my door and desperate to catch Thallia red handed in something nefarious, I stalk down the hall and open the door to Elijah's office without knocking.

Elijah stands suddenly at the intrusion, visibly relaxing when he sees it's me. "Lucy? Is everything okay?"

"I saw..." My voice catches in my throat, suddenly feeling silly for having barged in like this. What was I going to do? Accuse Thallia because she went into the woods?

"What did you see, baby?" He lifts an arm, beckoning me.

Walking around his desk so I'm standing next to him, he pulls me into his lap, nuzzling my neck.

Huffing out a breath, I relax into him. "I was looking out my window and saw all the warriors shift into wolves, running into the forest."

"It's the full moon," he says into my neck, and I can feel his eyelashes against my cheek. "Our wolves itch to run free and howl to the Moon Goddess."

"Do you get...stronger or anything?" I swallow as he starts slowly kissing my neck.

"Not really, no," he says between kisses, and my eyes close in bliss. "It's more like our wolves are closest to the surface on the full moon."

"Mmm-hmm," is all I can get out as I stretch my neck, allowing better access as his arms tighten around me.

"Is that all? You seemed kind of concerned."

"No..." Shaking my head and remembering why I came here, I pull back from him, meeting his eyes. "I saw someone...it looked like they were sneaking into the woods. Eli, I think..." A shuddering breath escapes me. He's not going to like this at all. "I think it was Thallia."

He frowns slightly before resuming the attention he was paying to my neck. "I'm sure she just wanted to go for a run with her wolf, Lu."

His lips on my neck feel like heaven, and I clench my thighs back. He's distracting me. "She was clothed," I counter, putting a hand on his chest to push him away from my neck. "I'm serious, Elijah, I think she's up to something."

"Not this again, Lucy." He rolls his eyes, making my blood boil. "We talked about this. Thallia isn't 'up to' anything."

Abruptly standing from him, I take a few steps back, breathing hard. "She was obviously the one responsible for the whole hot springs thing."

He stands as well, shaking his head. "She wouldn't do something like that."

"Actually, she's the only person I know in this pack who *would* do something like that," I argue. "Do you even pay attention when you talk to her? When she talks to me? She acts sweet, but there's venom in her words. Hidden insults. More than one time she's insinuated that I'm less-than for being human—"

"You don't know what you're talking about," he all but snarls. "You need to stop obsessing over her and figure out something better to do with your time."

His words are like a slap to the face. Laughing bitterly, I shake my head. "If I had come in here and told you *any other person* acted that way, you'd be at their throat. But you're blind when it comes to her." Before he can answer, I stomp out of the room, slamming his office door shut.

The next morning, I'm standing on my balcony, taking in the beautiful scenery. I'm snug in my sweater and jeans, my fur lined slippers keeping my toes warm.

"Hi, Luna!" Silvy Meyers, an adorable four year old with red pigtails, is skipping along the snow, her mother behind her. She keeps calling me Luna, even though I've told her quite a few times that I'm not Luna *yet*.

"Hi Silvy!" I call out. "Did you enjoy your rice krispy treats?"

"I did!" She skips to just below the balcony, turning her little cherub face up at me. "I liked the chocolate chip cookies too!"

I smile down at her, resting my elbows on the railing. "I'll have to make some more—ah!" The railing gives a small crack, causing me to jump backwards before the railing completely crumbled, falling from the building, right towards—

"Silvy!" her mother screamed. I scrambled forward, looking over the edge of the balcony. Breathing out a sigh of relief, I see Silvy's mother has snatched her out of the way of falling debris right in the knick of time.

Rushing down the stairs, I scramble out the front door, soaking my slippers in the snow. "Silvy, are you okay?!" I kneel down in front of her, turning to look at her mother who is shaking. "I'm so sorry—"

The mother shakes her head. "You couldn't have known that would happen. I've seen the Alpha lean on that railing plenty of times. I'm just glad I was here to pull her out of the way."

"Yeah, I'm okay, Luna!" Silvy tells me with a big smile on her face, completely unaware of what would have happened if her mother hadn't been there to save her.

"If you want to come inside, I can make you some of those chocolate chip cookies right now," I smile, despite wanting to cry at what could have happened.

"Mama, can we?" Silvy turns excitedly towards her mother.

Her mother nods tightly, and I lead the way to the kitchen, showing Silvy how to make my mom's famous chocolate chip cookies.

After all, it's the least I can do considering what happened. Her mother is acting like it's okay right now, but if she had gotten hurt... I have a feeling she wouldn't feel the same way.

The next afternoon, I'm at the pond where Elijah and I had our first date, practicing my ice skating like I have been the last couple days. I must say I think I'm getting a lot better. I'm just getting started on my figure eights when something catches my eye on a turn.

Whipping my head around, I'm faced with a black car rolling down the hill straight towards me. Heart thundering, I skate as fast as I can off the pond, throwing myself into the snow. Voices yell in the distance and get my attention as I lift my head, wiping snow from my hair and eyelashes. The car made contact with a mountain of snow on the other side of the pond, which brought it to a stop, partially burying it in the snow bank.

"Luna!" Someone shouts, and I'm being helped to my feet a moment later.

"What...what happened?" My voice trembles from shock.

The man who helped me up, a warrior named Cole, I believe, looked to someone behind him. Peering around him, I see

Laurent, one of the werewolves who helped Elijah 'escort' me here.

"We were wondering what the car was doing up near the houses when it should be in a garage offsite." He looks at me with guilt on his face. "One of us leaned on it, and it started rolling. It must have been in neutral or something." He swallowed, bowing his head down, "We're so sorry, Luna, we didn't mean to put you in danger."

"It's okay," I try to say bravely. "Thank you." I place what I hope is a comforting hand on his shoulder. He nods at Cole, and the two of them start to try to unbury the car from the snow.

Swallowing as I watch Laurent and Cole moving the snow, I can't help but envision what might have happened if I hadn't seen the car in time. This is my second near-death experience in two days. First, the railing and now this? I guess you could say it was a coincidence, but to me it seems like something else.

On top of that, there's the whole issue with the springs and then Thallia. Her words about enemies being everywhere flood my mind. The paranoia seeps in like a bitter sting as I take a seat on the bench and begin pulling off my skates.

I wish that I could take Elijah's advice and find some peace in this place. A purpose or perhaps a hobby even. Besides cooking that is. But every time I think I'm getting closer to something, it's like something stops me in my tracks and I'm hurdled backwards.

Trying to navigate the harsh reality that is my life.

Two days later, I'm with Bailey in the kitchen of the pack house, trying out a new pancake recipe.

"Oooh, add chocolate chips!" she exclaims, tossing the bag to me. I grin as I pour a generous amount into the batter. Stirring the mixture, I make sure to incorporate all the chips before I scoop out a small bite, and hand it to her to taste.

"Oh yeah." Her eyes nearly roll to the back of her head. "Give Eli a taste of this, and he'll rail you even harder than he normally does."

Choking on a laugh, I don't bother telling her that Elijah and I haven't had sex since before the full moon when I told him about my suspicions about Thallia and he blew me off. Again.

Moving to the stove to prep the pan, I turn on the heat when there's a loud popping sound that makes me jump backwards. "Shit!" I throw my hands up in an attempt to shield myself from the flames that engulf from the stove.

"Fuck!" Bailey yanks me back, before grabbing the fire extinguisher and putting out the flames.

"Don't burn yourself!" I cry, but she just smiles grimly at me and looks at the stove, which is no longer flaming, but looks like snow melted over it.

"Shifter healing." She runs her hand under the cold water of the sink. "Are you okay?"

Turning my arms, I check myself for injury. "Yeah, I'm okay."

Though with the way my heart is racing and panic has seeped in I don't think I'm mentally okay after this. There's no way that this is a coincidence too.

Nodding, she turns to the pancake batter and frowns. "Dammit, I was really looking forward to pancakes. We'll get someone out to fix the stove. It must be the gas line."

Gas line?

"Yeah," I reply, clearing my throat. "A gas line."

She hesitates for a moment, her brows furrowing as she takes a step towards me with concern in her gaze. "Is everything okay?"

"Yeah," I nod. Obviously lying. "Cereal it is?"

Two bowls and a cereal box later and the two of us are eating in silence. My mind plays over everything that's happened since I arrived. As much as I don't want to say anything to Bailey, she's the only one I feel like I can talk to right now.

"Hey, Bailey... can I ask you something?"

She laughs for a moment, before shoving a spoonful of cereal into her mouth. "Of course you can, what's on your mind?"

"What's Thallia's deal?"

She snorts at my question, her eyes wide as she drops her spoon and swallows her bite of food. "That bitch? What the fuck has she done now?"

Raising a brow, I take another bite. "You don't like her?"

"My dislike of her stems from petty childhood issues. Her parents died when she was young, and since her dad was close to my dad, we took her in. Well, she did not like the fact that my brother hung out with me, and clung to him constantly, which made Eli feel sort of responsible for her."

"How old was she when her parents died?"

"We were eleven and she was eight." Bailey rolls her eyes. "I tried to be friends with her, tried to be nice. But it was like she saw everything as a competition for Elijah's affections. Any time we were alone, she was snotty with me, tried to tell me that my own brother didn't want to hang out with me."

Sounds familiar.

"The bullshit only stopped when I joined warrior ranks and couldn't hang out with him anymore. He never believed me when I told him what she said anyway. I think he thought *I* was the jealous one."

"She's said some things to me too," I murmur, staring at my bowl. Elijah really was just blind when it came to this woman.

"Honestly, I think she always thought she would end up with him," Bailey continued, chewing, "but I would just ignore her now, Lucy. She doesn't have the balls to do anything to you—you've already won. You're his mate."

Despite the fact that her words were meant to reassure me, they only did one thing; confirm my suspicions about her feelings. The railing to my balcony breaking, the car that almost ran me over, and now the stove bursting into flames...I couldn't help but think that Bailey was wrong about one thing.

Thallia does have the balls to do something, and it might just cost me my life.

Chapter 17

Too Little, Too late

Lucy

I've spent the last three days in my room. Whenever Elijah would come to see me, I'd tell him I wasn't feeling well. I want to go downstairs, but something inside me—won't let me. My hand rests on the doorknob, and I stare at it, as if thought alone would overcome my fear and wrench the door open for me. I will my wrist to twist, but then flashes of the last couple of days enter my mind.

The balcony railing.

The car rolling down the hill.

The fucking stove nearly being engulfed in flames.

They can't all have been accidents. What if whoever is doing this has something else waiting for me? I miss Elijah. I want to mend things with him, maybe I can tell him everything that's been going on, and he'll finally take me seriously. I had asked Bailey and Laurent not to mention anything about the strange accidents to him, thinking more stress is the last thing he needs. Now though...the fact that I can't bring myself to leave my room...I think it's time to tell him. I just need to get through this fucking door.

I just can't bring myself to turn the knob.

What if the next one gets me, and Elijah never finds out what really happened? Then Thallia really could make a move on him...

No.

Fuck Thallia. Fuck whoever is coming after me. I need to show them that they don't run my life. Lifting my chin defiantly, I wrench my door open and step out into the hall. I don't even realize I'm holding my breath until I look at the hallway and see that it's empty, the air escaping me in relief.

My eyes seek Elijah's office...I can see the light under the crack of the door, so he's still working. I want to make things right with him, to make him happy. He's been so stressed about the rogue attacks recently.

An idea strikes me. Rushing down the stairs to check my ingredients in the kitchen, I grin when I see I have everything I need for the dessert I want to make.

Two hours later, I'm putting the finishing touches on a plate of macarons, which I haven't made in forever, but was my first truly difficult baking endeavor with my mom. Smiling at the memory, I remember how frustrated I had become on my fifth attempt to make perfect macarons. "Patience, my love," she had said to me, dabbing a pit of powdered sugar on my nose and making me giggle despite the tears threatening to break through. "Now you know that if you don't let them dry out for long enough, the steam will escape through the top and make cracks."

I had left Elijah out to dry for long enough. Hopefully, whatever we had...mate bond, love, who-the-hell-knows, wouldn't crack when put to the test. Finding a shiny metal serving tray in one of the cupboards, I place my plate on it, and slowly walk up the stairs. The last thing I want to do is drop my creation.

Wouldn't be able to blame anyone but myself for that one.

Standing outside his door, my heart thunders so loudly I'm sure everyone in the house can hear it. I can do this. It is only my heart and soul I have on a literal platter.

No biggie.

This was me trying to convey feelings without words the only way I know how. Elijah has always been so sure, so forthright. I never give an inch, let alone a mile. I want to do something to show him how much I care about him. I want him to know that with or without the mating bond, I was in this. That I'm here because of him, and nothing else. Without knocking, I gently open the door to the Elijah's office, only to be met with a sight that makes me want to vomit. Or scream. Or die.

You have got to be fucking kidding me.

Elijah is sitting in his chair, and there's a blonde woman sitting on his desk, leaning over him, with her lips planted firmly on his.

Fucking Thallia.

Angrily, I throw the tray on the floor, the evidence of my love and labor crashing to the ground. Before either of them can register what's happening, I turn, rushing down the hallway and into my room.

This must be what's been keeping him so busy the last couple of days. I bet there haven't been any rogue attacks either. Seething, I shake my head. I've been such an idiot. Of course he didn't really love me. I'm just pissed he made me fall for him.

Seeing red, I rush to my closet and find a bag, stuffing whatever I can into it. Grabbing the flashlight on my nightstand, I'm glad that at least Bailey seems to care about me enough to provide me with one. I only pause for my father's journals before I throw on my coat, hat, gloves, and boots, and hightail it out of there, slamming my door shut behind me.

Nobody is around to stop me as I race through the pack territory, aiming for the treeline I know we came through when I first came here. It's dark, but the light of my flashlight illuminates my path as I run, praying that I'm going in the right direction.

As I pass the fallen log that Elijah had roughly jumped over in an attempt to quiet me on the way to the pack, relief floods my chest.

I'm close.

I'm not stupid, I know that if he cared to come after me, he would have caught up with me already. That if Thallia and Elijah locking lips was an unwelcome come-on, he would have been shoving her away. It's just as Thallia had said.

He had grown bored of me. This was all a game to him. I bet Thallia was right when she said I might not even be his mate. What I feel when he touches me could just be hormonal, and I wouldn't know any better. I don't feel a *spark*. I'm just a stupid, useless human. Perfect to trick to get the only thing he wants—to become fully the Alpha.

What hope did I have against Thallia with her long legs, amazing figure, and a wolf form that probably oozes sex just like her human form does. I don't even have a wolf form.

Tears breach my tear ducts as I run further, the wind whipping my face. Despite my anger, I couldn't help but hope that I would hear his running footsteps behind me. Hope that he would catch me, take me in his arms, and tell me that she had a gun to his head or something and that's why he wasn't pulling away from her.

But no footsteps sound behind me, and no warm, strong hands pull me into an embrace. After what seems like forever, I finally arrive back at my father's cabin, wrenching the door open, and rushing inside. I don't bother starting a fire, opting to put my back against the locked door, sliding down it onto the floor in the darkness, quiet sobs wracking my body.

I don't know how long I'm sitting there, silently crying, before there's a knock on the door. "Lucy? Lucy, baby, are you in there?"

Elijah?

Sniffling, I wipe my eyes. "Go away."

I hear him sigh in what I might have once thought to be relief, but now I know better. "Lucy, sweetheart. I've been looking everywhere for you."

"I'm pretty sure you were too busy sucking face with Thallia to have been looking for me." My attempt at making my voice sound detached fails, and instead I sound like I might break into tears. Which, to be fair, is definitely the case.

"I...shit." He sighs, and there's slight creaking, followed by the sensation of the door that I'm resting against being slightly pushed back into me. He must be sitting on the floor against the door as well. "Can I tell you what happened?"

"I don't want a play-by-play of your hot makeout session," I snap, feeling angry that he was trying to explain anything to me.

Ignoring my answer, he tells me anyway, his voice slightly muffled by the door between us. "She came into my office, telling me about a trip she wants to take. She asked me to come with her," he paused, as if waiting for a comment from me. At my silence, he continues, "I told her that it wasn't appropriate for me to go on any trips with her now that I'm mated, and that I was hoping to take you somewhere nice at some point. Then...and I *swear*, I didn't even see it coming, she just kissed me. And I'm ashamed to admit it, but I froze."

Fucking sad excuse.

I hear his sigh and I can just picture him running his hands through his hair. "I froze because I grew up protecting this girl. I know making a move on me was unacceptable, but I also know I held her hand when she was ten because she was sad that her parents died. I know that we played tag as kids, and that I always thought I could trust her. I didn't know how to pull away without completely destroying all of that. I don't know if I ever led her on, but..." Another sigh escaped him.

"A loud noise helped me snap out of it, and I told her in no uncertain terms that what she did was unacceptable and that it would never happen again. Then I saw your macarons on the floor...I'm so sorry, Lu. I don't know alot about baking but I know those are bitch to make. Your door was closed and the light was off. I mindlinked the pack asking if they'd seen you, but nobody had. I checked the pond where we ice skated. It wasn't until I actually went into your room and saw your clothes missing from your closet that I figured out you ran. As soon as I pieced all that together I came straight after you."

Too little, too late.

My heart's broken. Elijah made me fall in love with him, but he was just using me.

"No." I shake my head even though he can't see it. "I don't believe you."

"Lucy—"

"No, Elijah! All I have done since you dragged me out against my will to your pack is try to make you happy! Try to belong to a place where I have no business being!" My breathing turns ragged as I stand, turning to face the door. "I have tried so hard to make this work with you..." I'm trying so hard not to start crying again. "But I almost died three times in the last week, and you didn't even check up on me! I bet that I'm not even really your mate!"

"What are you—"

"I'm talking!" I cut him off, nearly screaming. "You're an asshole, Elijah. You made me fall in love with you, when it turns out you were using me the whole time." Letting out a bitter laugh, a tear leaves my cheek and lands on the carpet. "What better way to pretend you found your mate than to fool a human who can't even feel it."

"Lucy, I—" This time he's cut off by my scream as I hear glass shatter in the kitchen. Before I can react further, a wolf enters the living room, and I retreat, bumping against the door.

"Baby, are you okay?" He's yelling in a panicked voice, jiggling the door.

I turn, trying to unlock it, but my hands are shaking so badly. "Elijah, help!"

"Shit!" I hear him exclaim before the sound of wolves snarling comes from the other side of the door.

"Easy there, sweet cheeks." The wolf had shifted into his human form while I wasn't looking and starts walking towards me with a vial of clear liquid attached to a needle.

"Elijah!" I scream, trying to run.

Silently cursing myself for separating from the one person who would have been able to protect me, I claw at the man as he snags me around the waist.

"Well, aren't you a pretty thing?"

"Fuck you," I spit, earning nothing but a laugh from him.

"Maybe the Rogue Alpha will let me have you when he's through with you." Before I can say anything, he plunges the needle into my neck. My body thrashes before everything starts to go fuzzy. The sound of wolves snapping at each other fills my ears as my body starts to go limp within the man's arms.

The world tilts, and with a muffled thud I land on the floor, everything going dark.

Chapter 18

Just Getting Started

Lucy

"Lucy! Lucy, I'll find you, just hold on!"

A memory of a voice echoes in my pounding head, and a groan escapes me as I try to open my eyes. My eyelids might as well be made of lead, and I panic, my breathing increasing rapidly. It feels like I'm laying on hard ground…maybe I'm laying on my side? There's painful pressure against my ribs and hip bone.

What happened?
Where am I?
Why can't I move?

I remember…walking in on Elijah and Thallia. I remember my heart thundering as I made a mad dash for my father's cabin. and Elijah trying to explain what happened.

My heart lurches. A rogue drugged me. Elijah couldn't get to me. Would he even *want* to get to me? I don't even know where I am. Trying to calm my racing mind, I focus on my other senses.

My hands are together, something digging into my wrists painfully. They must be bound together.

There are no voices, only the echo of water dripping periodically.

It smells…damp. And musty.

How much time has passed since they took me? My stomach turns as I try to open my eyes again. They feel less heavy than before, but I still don't get anywhere. Whatever they gave me must take more time to wear off.

What if someone is in the room with me right now?

Fuck.

Keeping my breathing regulated, I curse myself for my reaction to Elijah. His explanation had made sense, but I was too angry and hurt by him not coming after me immediately. In my heart, I know I feel the mate bond, but I'm struggling to correlate my heart with my mind.

Trying to open my eyes again, my heart rate picks up when I'm able to crack them open.

I'm in a…cave?

The floor—a dark gray stone, runs about ten feet before the floor disappears entirely, creating a chasm between me and the narrow strip of rock that lines the opposite wall. As I crane my neck, I see a high, natural ceiling full of stalactites. Not having use of my hands makes things difficult, but I'm able to roll from my side onto my ass, sitting up and scanning the area.

The space that I'm in is empty. Semi-circular in shape, a narrow strip of ground running around the rounded circumference of the chamber, a ten foot chasm separating the island of land I'm on from the ground against the wall. Whipping my head around, I see that it's not an island I'm on, but a section of stone that narrows to a natural bridge, which leads to a giant chair against one of the walls. The wall the chair is against is not curved, but straight, with tunnels leading out on either side. There's no sunlight to be seen. I must be deep in a set of caves.

Looking closer at the chair, I realize that it's not really a chair at all, but a throne. Crudely made of bones and metal, it sits across the bridge like a dark omen, an unsettling indication of why I was here. I remember what the rogue who took me said.

"Maybe the Rogue Alpha will let me when he's through with you."

Swallowing, I try my wrists again. Maybe they underestimated my strength because I'm a human. Wincing at the friction of the rope, I realize they may have overestimated my strength. There's no way I can get out these restraints by myself.

But there's no one here...maybe I can sneak out before—

"You're up! Good, good," a deep, sinister voice calls, and my heart sinks as I notice the figure emerging from one of the tunneled pathways. I don't have a chance to say anything before he continues, "we weren't sure how much of the drug to give you, especially since you're human, and I'm not sure what side effects there will be, but it's not like it really matters."

He settles on the throne in front of me, elbows on his knees, and stares at me, his gaze filled with disdain, and something else I don't quite recognize.

"Who are you? What do you want?" My voice shakes in a way that I hate.

A sinister grin erupts on the man's face. He's probably in his mid-thirties, with brown hair, scars on his face, and red eyes. "I'm Alpha Leon. Alpha to the Rogue wolves of Alaska. I just wanted to see what was so special about a human that the future Alpha of the Blood Moon pack would sully himself with the lesser species."

Fury whips within me, and I have to restrain myself from going off on this man.

"Now that you're awake, and I see the fire in your eyes, I can see the appeal." He nods to himself as he sits back, lounging in his throne. He apparently doesn't require any sort of answer from me because he continues, chuckling. "I *was* just going to kill you, but no...no. Now, when Elijah inevitably comes to rescue you, I'll incapacitate him, and make him watch as I take you as my chosen mate."

My gut turns.

I think I'm gonna be sick.

"You...you can't," I say, sounding more confident than I feel.

"What makes you think you have any say in what I can or cannot do, human?" he sneers at me.

"I'm already his mate. Elijah's fated mate. I don't know a whole lot about the Moon Goddess, but I don't think she would allow a human to have two mates."

He bares his teeth in a smile that is anything but friendly. "You're right, you don't know anything about the Moon Goddess because if you did, you would know that your mate bond is practically worthless until you formally accept it. Which you obviously haven't, because there is no mate mark anywhere on you." My eyes widen as he leans forward again, his voice sending unwelcome shivers down my spine. "Believe me, I checked."

All I can do is whisper, "why are you doing this? What have I ever done to you to deserve this?"

He shrugs. "You are loved by the bastard responsible for *my* fated mate's death. An eye for an eye and all that."

He pushes himself from the throne, sauntering across the bridge that connects us. Kneeling in front of me, he runs a knuckle across my cheek. "Your *mate*," he sneers the word, "let all the other attackers from our ambush run away, except my darling Nora. Her, he killed in cold blood, just because of her connection to me. Do you think that's fair?"

"She must not have run when she was given the chance. Maybe she *wanted* to die to escape the agony of being your mate," I sneer, not sure what's come over me.

Stars dance in my vision as my head snaps to the side from the strike Leon lands on cheek. Groaning, I try to stay upright, and see him wiping the back of his hand on his shirt. "Ew, human blood."

Asshole.

"Get used to the idea, little spitfire because you're becoming my mate whether you want to or not, and I will not provide death as an easy way out for you." He sits back down in his throne, my cheek still throbbing from his strike. I can feel something warm and sticky where his hand had been. Did he split my skin open when he hit me?

"You have to know that you can't just make me be your mate. If Elijah has to wait for me to accept it as a fated mate, then—"

"Traditionally, yes, fated mate bonds are more powerful than chosen mate bonds. The offspring would be more powerful, the connection more intense. The issue of me not being able to force you...it might have been the case if you were a wolf shifter, little spitfire, but you're not. You're a human. If you were a wolf shifter, your wolf could protect you from any forced mating. But since you are completely defenseless, I will mark you, and I will seal the deal with roughest fuck you've ever had." His sinister grin returns. "And I'll make Elijah watch the whole thing."

This time, when the feeling of sickness comes, I can't stop it as I hunch over, dry heaving. Luckily there's nothing in my stomach—I have no idea how much time has passed since I was taken or when I last ate.

This is it. Even if Elijah does come for me, he'll be trapped and made to watch as Leon forces himself on me. When I finally got the dry heaving to stop, I noticed Leon looking at me with a sickeningly delightful look in his eyes.

"Stitches!" he calls, his eyes never leaving mine. A huge muscular man enters from the tunnel opposite of the one Leon came through.

"Stitches is going to entertain you while we wait for your Alpha Charming to get here," licking his lips, he leans forward yet again, "let's see how long it takes to douse you, little spitfire."

Stitches licks his lips, a demented expression on his face. His short blonde hair is shaved on the sides, and his red eyes are trained on me as he strides toward me. I do my best to scramble backwards, despite my hands being tied in front of me and being stuck on my ass.

"No! No!" I scream as he grasps my legs and pulls me towards him. "Please, Leon, please! I'll do anything you want!"

This makes Stitches pause, his head leaning towards Leon in

deference. Leon only sighs. "It's *Alpha* Leon. And...this is what I want."

Viewing this as a green light, Stitches reaches for the top of my pants and screeching, I put everything I can into a swing at his face with my tied hands. His head snaps to the side, and he looks back at me, pupils blown. My scream is muffled as he strikes me back across the face, the opposite side that Leon hit.

Despite the pounding in my head and the stars littering my vision, I kick my feet as wildly and hard as I can.

I won't let him rape me. I can't.

Another scream escapes me as Stitches gives up wrestling control of my legs, and morphs his nails into sharpened wolf claws. He rips my pants open with his sharp claws, and I gasp for air, crying out, "Elijah! Elijah, please help me!" I can see Leon laughing at me from his throne.

Please. Please. Please.

I clench my legs together defensively, but Stitches doesn't reach for my panties like I expect him to. Catching my movement, he sneers at me, "you really think I'd want to fuck human trash?"

I don't even have a second to be relieved because he takes his sharp nail that he used to cut off my pants, and runs it along my thigh, creating a swirling pattern of blood and pain. An ear shattering scream erupts from my chest as he continues carving into my flesh. My vision starts to go hazy, and I swear I can see Stitches licking his lips as he works wordlessly, my screams only seeming to egg him on. Before long, I'm reduced to a sobbing mess, wondering what Elijah will think of me when he finds me. Maybe he won't even want me anymore.

My body feels like it's on fire. It's so intense that it's hard to separate the old pain from the new pain. "Please...Elijah..." my voice rasps, spent from all of the screaming. I don't know if I can fight it anymore. Staring at the ceiling of the cave, I almost wish that one of the stalactites would fall and put me out of my misery.

Suddenly, Leon's face appears above mine, his hand wiping the tears from my face. My eyes flutter close, and the last thing I hear before welcoming the darkness is, "don't worry, little spitfire. We're just getting started."

Chapter 19

Reeks of a Trap

Elijah

Shit.

 Shit shit shit *shit*.

 This is all my fault. How could I have let them take her? I promised to keep her safe, and the first time she steps foot outside the pack, she gets kidnapped. If those two assholes hadn't shown up to keep me busy while the one inside the house took her, then I would have just knocked down the door.

 They had someone in human form that managed to hit me with a tranq, knocking me out. That was concerning enough, considering regular animal tranquilizers aren't enough to knock out a wolf shifter. I'd figure that one out later.

 The sun was just rising as I came to, and I immediately took off after the tracks in the snow. The whole thing reeks of a trap. Them leaving me alive, tranqing me instead of trying to kill me, and not dosing me enough to keep me out long enough for the tracks to be snowed over...they obviously want me to come after her.

 I'd play into their trap, and I'd make them regret it.

 My wolf is restless as I follow the tracks through, and eventually, it's clear they shift from wolf to human, and I look up to see myself at the base of a mountain. I follow the human tracks around a bend, to a small cave opening.

This is where they took her?

Closing my eyes and concentrating, I try to sense any other wolves. Their presences are faint, but they're there. If this is the base, it's disconcerting how close they are to the pack as well as Lucy's cabin. No wonder they could attack us so frequently.

"Riftan, I need you and some warriors. They took Lucy," I mindlink to Riftan. This is something I would only trust my Beta with.

"Shit. We're coming. Where are you?"

I give him directions using landmarks and Lucy's cabin as a starting point. *"I'm going in, meet me inside."*

His voice sounds concerned. *"Maybe you should wait until we get there, it might be a trap—"*

"I know it's a trap, but my mate is in there. I'm not going to sit around while they do Goddess-knows-what to her," I snarl, my wolf growling in my mind.

I can almost hear him sigh. *"I know. You're right...just be safe, Eli."*

I peer into the cave, bracing myself for someone to see me. Thankfully, it's empty though. After about twenty feet, the cave becomes illuminated, torches line the walls making everything a lot easier—except for hiding. Keeping close to the wall, I move as quietly as I can.

Where is everyone?

My worries are eased as I keep on down the tunnel, and come across branches in the tunneling system, each leading down hallways that curve off and disappear, no end in sight. My ears twitch, picking noise further down the tunnel that keeps to the left. At the noise, my wolf struggles against me, eager to be let loose and rip apart anyone who would dare to even look at my mate the wrong way, let alone drug and kidnap her.

At least, I assumed they drugged her based on the lack of

cursing and screaming that was present the last time someone dragged her from her cabin...

Me.

Usually I'm in complete control of my wolf, but Lucy being kidnapped has brought out a feral side of him that rivals even my rage at the situation. I don't know if it's because she's my mate, or because my wolf has practically been belly-up for her since we met her, but either way, he's too riled up to think anything through at the moment.

Keeping as close to the cave wall as possible, I creep towards the source of the noise. I would shift into my wolf, but I don't think I can trust him to not recklessly rush in and completely blow my cover.

The noise steadily grows louder, it sounds like multiple men talking loudly, but I can't make out anything specific, like multiple conversations are going at once. Soon, I see light pouring out of a break in the wall I'm following. The light shines against the wall opposite of the opening, and if the shadows are any indication, I got here right at breakfast time.

Shadows of multiple men fall against the wall, sitting at long tables, now that I'm closer, I can start to make out bits of conversation. Despite knowing that their conversation will mask any sound my steps make, I keep the slow pace until I'm able to peek around the wall into the room.

My wolf lurches at the sight of them and I push him down in a desperate bid to regain control. There's about fifteen of them, all sitting at one long table and eating together. They might look like any other pack sharing a meal together if it weren't for their red eyes.

I press my back against the wall and listen, hoping for any indication of where they might be keeping Lucy.

One voice sticks out to me. "We really should be increasing security, that Alpha will be coming after his mate soon."

Another one barks a laugh. "Oh please, we tranq-ed him enough that he'll be out at least another six hours."

A female voice next. "What if snow covers the tracks before he wakes? Then Alpha Leon won't be able to follow through with his plan if that other Alpha can't find us."

My gut clenches at the mention of a plan, and my wolf again attempts to overtake me. What is the Rogue Alpha planning to do with my mate?

"Clear skies, baby, clear skies. It's not supposed to snow until tonight," the original voice answers. At least I was right about it being a trap. The fact that I woke up sooner than they were expecting gives me an advantage.

"Screw increasing security," a new voice chimes in, "I mean, how much of a threat can this so-called Alpha be if he chose a *human* for a mate?"

"I've never been so inclined towards humans, but that bitches' screams were music to my ears," an oily voice chuckles.

My vision goes red. They have my mate, and they're torturing her...making her scream. My body starts to shake in rage, and just as I'm about to let my wolf out and do whatever the hell he wants to these sick, twisted fuckers, when Riftan mindlinks me. *"We'll take care of these fucks. You go get your mate."*

Whirling, I come face to face with Riftan, and ten warriors, including my sister and Laurent, behind him. They each nod at me, and before I turn, I link to all of them. *"Make them pay."*

I dart across the opening, and break into a run, not knowing exactly where I'm going but I can hear Lucy's screams.

The fight breaks out behind me as Riftan, Bailey, and Laurent lead the other seven wolves into battle, snarls and growls filling the air as they wreak havoc.

Not long after the battle behind me starts, Lucy's screams cut off, and I push myself harder, desperate to find her. I come to a large opening, a throne to my left, and what looks like a runway of rock, leading to a large platform.

There are three figures by the throne, along with the Rogue Alpha, with my mate clenched tightly to his side. My wolf snarls and howls at the sight of her, unconscious, the Rogue Alpha with his arms around her. Her pants are shredded and angry lines of red dance along the skin of her legs.

At the sight of the blood dripping down her thighs, I allow my wolf to break through, snarling and snapping, launching at the third figure; the one with his hands transformed into wolf claws and blood dripping from the tips. He runs towards me, completely transforming into wolf form, which is just as bulky and burly as his human form. He's bigger than I am, which is rare, and I come to the conclusion that he must not be very smart if he's this big but not the Alpha.

Dodging his initial attack, I leap to the side as he barrels past me, straight into the wall of the cave. Jingling above me catches my attention, and I quickly glance up at the stalactites on the ceiling.

Those could be useful.

I let out a snarl, and charge into him, bashing him against the wall, causing the stalactites to tremble again. He catches me by surprise, his maw capturing the scruff of my neck and slamming me down on the ground. Twisting to my back, I slide partially away from the wall, as he steps over me, thinking I've submitted to him.

"No, Stitches!" Leon warns, and I push all four of my legs against him, launching him against the cave wall a final time. He doesn't have time to stand before three stalactites fall from above, impaling him completely through his neck, abdomen, and haunches.

Turning my attention towards Leon, I stalk towards him, only hesitating because he has Lucy in his grasp. She slowly blinks her eyes open and focuses on me. "Elijah!" she calls out weakly, gasping in pain.

A growl rumbles in my chest as I zero in on Leon. "Now, now, don't be like that," he sneers, holding Lucy closer as she whines in pain. "You killed my mate, so it's only fair that you give me yours."

Being in my wolf form, I can't exactly answer him, but he

continues, "you know, she did call for you. While she was being... entertained. Pretty little tears ran down her cheeks when she realized you weren't coming for her. I'll make her feel wanted." He opens his mouth, baring his teeth dangerously close to her neck when I realize what he's about to do—he's going to claim her.

My wolf launches at Leon, who lets Lucy fall to the side. She's awake enough to scramble away as Leon shifts into his wolf. His wolf is brown, with silver streaked through, scars littering his body. He looks like hell.

Tackling Leon to the ground, my wolf is in a frenzy of bloodlust. To make him pay for hurting our mate. To make him hurt like she hurt. Leon and I grapple for the upper hand for a moment, rolling around at the foot of the throne—he's strong, I'll give him that. But the sound of Lucy's weeping in pain in the background is all the motivation my wolf needs.

My jaw clamps around Leon's throat. Not just the loose skin that I might use to toss him around, but his windpipe, his bones. He struggles for a moment as my teeth sink into his flesh before a whimper of submission escapes him, but it's too late for that. If I let him go, he'll only rebuild his forces and come back at us. Lucy will always be in danger.

No.

Leon signed his own death sentence when he kidnapped and tortured my mate.

With a loud snarl, I grip his throat, pulling my head back as hard as I can to rip it out. Shakily, I step back from Leon's corpse, blood dripping from my mouth. Shifting back into my human form, I hurry towards Lucy, who is in a heap next to the throne. I gently lift her up my arms under her knees and her head resting on my shoulder.

Tears sting my eyes as I look at her face, her eyes hallow, her hair a tangled mess. "It's okay, Lucy. I got you, baby, it's over now."

Her eyes blink open, red from her pain and her crying, and

she places a palm against my cheek. Leaning into it, I close my eyes and take a shuddering breath.

"You came for me..." A small, gentle smile is on her lips, and it's all I can do not drop to my knees in gratitude for saving my mate.

"I'll always come for you, Lucy. I love you."

Chapter 20

No Time to Relax

Elijah

She looks so peaceful. No one would ever think that mere hours ago she was kidnapped and tortured by rogue wolves inside of a mountain. I swallow, grasping her hand in mine as I look at her sleeping form in the hospital bed.

Her telling me that I found her was the only lucid thing she had said since I brought her out of that cave and rushed her to the small hospital in a nearby town. We don't have a full on hospital on pack lands, but we do keep a shifter-specific doctor on our payroll at the local hospital for situations like this.

They immediately stitched up the gashes in her legs, and currently had her on an antibiotic drip and pain meds. Due to the state of her pants when I brought her in, the first thing they did after stitching her up was check for any signs of sexual assault. It felt like a weight was lifted off my chest when they said that there was no sign of distress on that part of her body.

Yet, regardless of knowing that it still kills me that she was hurt.

She's sleeping, which they say is normal and expected, but it doesn't stop me from feeling her pulse every couple of hours. Dr. Sullivan is standing at the foot of her bed with a clipboard while a nurse checks her vitals.

"So, she'll be okay?" My voice wavers and I hate it. I'm supposed to be confident, unshakeable. I need to be strong for Lucy. Stay with her, make sure she makes a full recovery. I feel so helpless, which is not something I'm used to feeling as the Alpha. Any sleep I get is restless, hunched over the side of her bed, my head by her lap.

"She'll make a full recovery, Alpha, don't worry." He nods kindly at me. "She'll have a hard time walking, probably, and will be in pain, but eventually it will be like it never happened." He swallows. "Well, except for the scarring."

"The scarring?" I echo, my voice concerned.

"These weren't clean cuts," he explains, pushing his glasses up on his nose. "The wolf shifter who made these marks used their claws, not a knife. If it had been clean cuts, there would have been minimal scarring. But these will not be pretty to look at, and it may cause her to revisit the trauma when she looks at them."

My poor Lucy. How did we get here?

After Doctor Sullivan leaves, I try to get some rest, laying my head on her bed, holding her hand. As much as I want to stay awake, ensuring that she's safe, I can't. The exhaustion of everything finally overtaking me as my eyes close and I succumb to the darkness calling me.

I'm awoken to the feeling of fingers running through my hair, and my eyes peek open, only to see Lucy staring off into space as she gently strokes my head. She hasn't noticed me yet, and I take the opportunity to look her over.

Dark circles are under her normally bright eyes, and her hair, a limp mess. She has a cut above her cheek, and her expression is dull...lifeless. She looks like she's been through hell and back.

"How do you feel?" Her eyes jump to me at the sound of my voice, but I keep my head down in hopes that she continues running her fingers across it.

"I've been better," she admits, her eyes roaming over my face. "The doctor said—"

"I know." She gives a sad smile. "You've been asleep a while. He came in and told me."

"Can I—" Clearing my throat, I lift my head from the bed. "Can I explain everything to you?"

She nods silently, her gaze empty. "Thallia's parents were warriors. They both died protecting Riftan and I. We wandered out into the woods when we weren't supposed to when we were eleven, and rogues attacked. We were lucky Thallia's parents were patrolling nearby and heard our screams. They were outnumbered two to four, and we didn't have our wolves yet. By the time my dad got there and finished off the rogues, they had sustained too many injuries. They died that night."

Shame fills me, and I don't dare meet Lucy's eyes. "My parents raised Thallia as a result. My dad always made sure I knew it was my fault, and drilled it into me that she was my responsibility because it was my fault her parents died. I protected her, played with her, let her hang out with my friends and me. I didn't realize how possessive she had become. Looking back, I see it...but at the time, I was just focused on doing what my dad told me to. Taking responsibility for my actions and all that."

She grasps my hand reassuringly, silently encouraging me to continue. Taking a shaky breath, I let the words spill out of me. "Shortly after my dad died, she tried to kiss me. I thought maybe she was caught up in the grief of losing her father figure. I explained that I didn't look at her that way, that she was like a sister to me. Not only that, but I just found out I had to find my fated mate. She seemed to take it well, and we never spoke of it again. I only realized she had never moved on when she kissed me in my study."

Tears blur my vision at the hurt that I know I've caused Lucy, and she gives me a moment to collect myself before I continue. "I'm sorry I didn't move right away, Lu. That I didn't shut her down immediately. But it was like I was frozen, my brain was sending all these thoughts to my body, but I was stuck. I knew what I wanted to do, I wanted to push her away. But all I could hear was my dad's voice in my head telling me that I need to take responsibility for her." Sighing, I rub the back of my neck. "I know it's inexcusable, Lucy. But I would never intentionally hurt you. I love you."

"Thank you for telling me." Her voice is quiet. "I understand, that must have been difficult for you." I try to ignore the fact that she didn't say that she loves me back. She's quiet for a moment, but then says, "but...it will be different now, right? You see that she has feelings for you, so you'll distance yourself from her?"

Nodding, I rub my jaw. "Yeah. We'll have to put some firm boundaries in place. I'm sorry I didn't take you seriously before, Lu."

"It's okay...I'm just glad she showed her true colors," Lucy says, smiling sadly at me. "Even if she kissed you, I'm glad the truth is out there now and we can all move forward."

"Me too, Lu." I reply, pressing a kiss to the back of her hand. "Me too."

The next day, I'm walking back to Lucy's room from finalizing the paperwork with the front desk when Doctor Sullivan catches me.

"Elijah," he says, dropping formalities due to the human setting we're in. "I was just speaking to Lucy and told her all of her discharge information. The stitches will dissolve on their own, and I've prescribed her a course of antibiotics just to be safe. I have a visit scheduled with her in four weeks to..." He stops, shaking his head. "Forgive me. My thoughts have been everywhere lately. As I said, I have a visit scheduled in four weeks to check to make sure her wounds are healing properly."

After rattling off some more information about how to keep her comfortable, he goes on his way, and I crack open Lucy's door. She's watching some cable home improvement show on the TV on the wall. Well, her head is turned towards the TV but I can't tell if she's actually absorbing any of it.

"Sweetheart?" I call out, not wanting to startle her, and she turns towards me. "You get to go home today, are you ready?" She nods, and I bring out a sweatshirt and a pair of sweatpants that I bought at the gift shop downstairs. She doesn't speak, just lets me move her arms and legs around like she's a doll that I'm dressing.

Once she's dressed, I take a step back. "Are you okay?"

My voice seems to shake her out of whatever trance she is in, because she nods. "I'm fine, Eli, just tired." She smiles weakly at me.

She doesn't *look* fine. She looks like hell. I want nothing more than to wrap her in my arms and kiss the answers out of her. I want to lay her body down and worship her, erase every bad memory she's had embedded in her soul the last twenty-four hours.

But I won't.

I'll give her time to process everything she's been through, and when she's ready to talk, I'll listen. The fact that she's still standing after everything she went through is just a testament to how right the Moon Goddess was in making her my mate.

"Thallia needs to be moved," I tell Riftan, "away from me, away from Lucy. That shit she pulled can't happen again."

He nods. "Of course."

"Give her the old Flagwell home. It's been empty long enough. That should keep her from coming up with any sort of excuse to come see me." Leaning in closer, I add, "and keep an eye on her. You, one of the warriors, whoever. Some weird shit is going on, and I want to know what it is. I need you to be my eyes, Rif."

"I'll let her know right away, and I'll get my men on it," he agrees. He turns to leave, but then quickly stops in his tracks and turns back to face me. "How's Lucy doing?"

Looking up to her balcony, which is in clear view from where I'm standing in front of the pack house with Riftan, I see the light of her TV through the glass doors. "As well as she can be expected, considering the circumstances. We're on the third *Lord of the Rings* movie."

Lucy and I got back midmorning, after a short trip from the hospital back to pack territory. Using vehicles isn't something we do often. One, because of the terrain. And two, usually we're in wolf form everywhere we go. However, in this case...the old pick up truck I got when I was a teen came in handy.

We settled her in her room with a pop-up tray for her meals and any movie she can possibly imagine watching. She had insisted that she could walk down the stairs for meals, but I wasn't having any of it. The only thing I want her to do is to rest.

She seemed to realize I was on to something, because she was munching on chips, popcorn, and sipping on a soda when I came down here to talk to Riftan.

"One last thing, Rif," I say once the conversation starts wrapping up. "I don't...don't tell anyone about what she went through. She doesn't want anyone to know the details. They can just know that she was taken but that we rescued her."

Riftan nods grimly, and I go back into the pack house, taking the steps two at a time to get back to Lucy's room. The moment I get there, I hesitate, peeking through the crack of the door before making myself known. She tries to put on a brave face for me, but when I see her when she doesn't know I'm looking—unguarded, unfiltered, and raw—that's when I can tell what she's really thinking.

It started out unintentionally. After we went ice skating the first time, I noticed that her features were more relaxed if I wasn't looking at her. I don't think she even does it consciously, just conditioned by years of trying to make herself as small as possible so she didn't inconvenience the ones tasked with raising her.

Her brows are knit together, her lips pursed. She has that line at the top of the bridge of her nose that appears whenever she's thinking hard about something. The movie is paused, and she's turned the light on the side table, a thick, sturdy looking book propped on her lap. "The Anatomy of Wolves" is on the cover. My brows furrow, and I crack the door open a little more, making her jump.

"Hey, Sweetheart. You paused the movie for me?" I ask as I climb back on the bed with her.

"Oh. Yeah," She glances at the TV like she forgot it was even on. "Just reading a little bit."

"Oh?" I raise a brow. "Brushing up on your wolf anatomy? I didn't even think we had books like that here."

She flushes, closing the book before putting it on her nightstand. "You don't. When we got here, I asked Bailey if she could run to my dad's cabin and grab it. She brought it up a minute after you went outside to talk to Riftan."

"Any reason you're reading up on wolf anatomy? Not trying to figure out the best way to kill me, are you?" I grin at her, and she chuckles.

"No. I just thought it might be useful to know now that I'm living among all of you."

Seems reasonable enough.

When she sees I'm satisfied with her answer, she grabs the remote. "Want to keep watching?"

Nodding, I settle into the bed. "Yeah. It'll be time for your pain meds when this ones done."

We finish the night watching some more movies, and read our own respective books for about an hour before we turn off the lights. She's definitely more at ease than she was back at the hospital, but I'm still a bit concerned about how distracted and jumpy she is.

She's definitely handling things better than I thought. But deep down, I know the truth. It's all a facade to her. She's screaming on the inside, and she thinks nobody is listening.

Chapter 21

Stupid, Stupid, Stupid

Lucy

I'm so tired.

It's been two weeks since Elijah brought me home from the hospital, and though my legs are almost completely healed, sometimes my dreams turn to nightmares as phantom pains plague my thighs and calves. Images of that monster torturing me rack every second of the darkness that tries to overcome me from exhaustion. And though deep down I know I'm safe...I feel like a prisoner in this world.

Unable to move on. Unable to feel happiness.

Whenever I wake in a cold sweat, my heart racing and ears ringing, I try to stay as quiet as possible so I don't disturb Elijah sleeping next to me as I trace my fingers down the raised, red flesh of my legs.

It was just a dream. It's over now. It was just a dream.

That's my mantra as I breathe in through my mouth and out through my nose, closing my eyes as I focus on the sensation of my skin against the source of my nightmares. As much as I try to not wake Eli, he always seems to know when I'm up anyway, and often puts me back to sleep by running his hands through my hair as I lay down or rubbing my back.

For the first time in two weeks, Elijah has left my side for more than an hour, and I finally have some room to breathe and process everything. It's not like I haven't enjoyed his attentiveness and company. In fact, I revel in it. It allows me to try and feel safe, to feel like I'm not alone for the first time in a very long time.

Today, when he left my room, he explained that he had put off his duties as Alpha for too long, and Riftan was 'really up his ass' to get back to work and review the warrior patrol schedule now that the rogues are gone.

Now, I'm sitting in a chair by my window, gazing at the pack grounds below me. My hand caresses my lower stomach, and I sigh, remembering how the doctor came to me with blood work results while Elijah was filling out paperwork at the front desk. I realize now that I shouldn't have been so surprised—I haven't had my period since coming here. He put me at about 5 weeks pregnant, which means I'm now roughly 7 weeks along.

It must have happened the very first night we had sex back at my cabin. Between arguing with Elijah, and trying to survive. Not that it really matters anyways. The pill isn't 100% effective against pregnancy.

Stupid, stupid, stupid.

I begged the doctor to not tell Elijah yet. I told him I wanted to surprise him, but I didn't truly know why I was so against Elijah knowing...fear, shock, or something else altogether, but now I know.

I don't want him to come looking for me.

Among the general first-time-pregnancy information Doctor Sullivan gave me, he also told me that human-werewolf interbreeding wasn't something that was done often, but enough for us to know that there is a 50/50 chance the baby could be a were—shifter, as the pack people keep calling it. On the other side of that...the child could also be human.

It's not something I had been planning on until I had time by myself to think, but now that I've had some uninterrupted time... I'm going to leave Elijah. The pack. Alaska. I have too. If there's even a sliver of a chance that this baby is going to be human, I'm not going to raise them in an environment as dangerous as this one where they don't have any way to protect themselves.

And even if they do end up being a shifter...that has to diminish their strength somewhat, if their mother is a human.

I don't *want* to leave. I think I might even love Elijah. But I need to put the baby first. I know first hand how dangerous this place can be. And even though I've been told that the Rogues have been taken care of, what if there are more?

The guy from the cave was so sure of himself. Rogue Alpha of all, he said. Or at least, that's what I remember. What if he was only a portion of them. I mean, this is Alaska.

What if some rogue wolf creates another pack and starts attacking again? Elijah and his pack *did* kill the rogue *Alpha*. Surely, there are going to be others from his pack that weren't killed and are pissed wanting revenge.

I may be naive to the way Elijah and his people live, but I'm not stupid. I've seen enough movies to know that there's always someone. Something that can happen. I know Elijah wants to protect me, and that he would love the baby fiercely, but in the end, is love enough to keep them safe?

Shaking my head and standing, my resolve strengthens. I'll leave, somehow, and raise the baby. If they start showing signs of being a shifter...then I'll let them decide if they want to come back.

My hands glide over my stomach again, and I breathe out, closing my eyes. It breaks my heart to think that Elijah won't ever know his baby, but the baby's safety is more important than how he or I feel. I don't want to leave him. But it isn't about us. It's about our child. The love that I already feel for this life growing inside me is something that not even the mate bond can rival.

A wave of nausea rolls through me, and I still myself, breathing through my nose. I haven't actually vomited yet, but it's difficult to hide the feelings of nausea that periodically overtake me. I would have to leave soon before Elijah starts to notice. Besides my aching breasts, the random waves of nausea are my only pregnancy symptom.

Knowing I need a plan, I start with how to get out of Alaska. The solicitor set everything up for me coming out, but I would be on my own for the way back.

I would need money for a plane ticket, and even though I hate the thought of taking anything from Elijah, I'm sure he has cash stashed somewhere.

But what will I do when I get back to Rhode Island?

Shaking my head, I turn to pace the room. No, I can't go back to Rhode Island. That would be the first place he'd look for me if he comes after me. Maybe Ohio? Or Wisconsin. Somewhere that I can get a job under the table to get a cheap place for me and the baby.

Slow down, Lucy, first things first. How am I going to get off pack territory without anyone finding out?

I would have to find a way to sneak out of the house undetected, then get to the nearest airport. No, that wouldn't work. I could hardly make the hike before my legs were damaged and exhaustion from growing a human life took over. Maybe there are snowmobiles stashed somewhere? Snowmobiles are a thing, right? I'm trying to think of where they would keep the snowmobiles if they have them, when I'm interrupted by a light knock on the door.

"Elijah?" My brow furrows as I take him in, leaning against the door frame of my open door, a box stuffed under his arm. "What's that?" I ask, pointing to the box.

"I was hoping you could tell me." To anyone who didn't know him, the statement might have sounded lighthearted, but there's an undertone of tenseness there that makes the hairs on my arms raise. His blue eyes that are normally filled with such warmth and love look almost cold now. "Riftan brought this to me." His tone gives nothing away as he walks to the bed, placing the box on the end. The flaps are slightly raised, indicating that it's been opened already.

What could be in the box?

What would make him act like this? Is there a threat on my life? Did one of the Rogues survive and threaten me? Is this more of Thallia's games?

Slowly walking to the bed, the label on one of the flaps of the box catches my eye. My name.

"Opening my mail?" I ask, feeling combative but trying to keep the indignation from my voice.

"Everyone's packages get opened as a security measure," he answers just as evenly.

"Everyones? Or just mine?"

"Anyone who is at risk for an attempt on their life."

"You said all the rogues were killed."

"That doesn't mean I'll start being careless with my mate's life."

Steeling myself, I peer into the box.

My blood runs cold.

On a bed of foam peanuts, is a bottle of prenatal vitamins, a tea to prevent nausea, and an ointment to soothe aching breasts. My breathing goes shallow, as I pick up the note on the top, and read the doctors handwriting,

Lucy,

Here is a small care package to get you started. I'll be by for a check-in in about 2 weeks.

-Dr. Sullivan

Tears burn my eyes. It's ruined. All of it. Now that he knows, he'll never let me go. When I place the note back in the box, sure that he's already read it, I meet his eyes.

Elijah stills.

"It's true?" He chokes out, and my heart breaks at the betrayal lining his voice. I try to form the words, to tell him I'm sorry for not telling him, but nothing comes out. "I can't believe..." He shakes his head. "How long have you known?" he demands, leaning toward me.

"Doctor Sullivan told me at the hospital." I admit, my voice barely a whisper.

"Two weeks?" His voice raises. "Two fucking weeks, Lucy? Why didn't you tell me?"

A feeble excuse leaves me. "I was waiting—"

"Don't fucking give me that! We've been together 24/7 the last two weeks, you can't say that you were waiting for the right time."

Staring at him, my gaze hard, I move to sit on the bed.

"Why didn't you tell me?" he demands again.

"Because you never had to know, okay?" My voice seems to echo in the distance between us, and a look of shock registers on his face.

"What do you mean?" he asks slowly, deliberately, as if giving me a chance to fix the mistake I just made. But it wasn't a mistake. It was the truth.

"I was planning on leaving." I refuse to back down. He has to see reason in this, that this pack is no place for a baby that might be human.

"You would..." I almost flinch at the sound of his voice breaking. "You would take my baby from me?"

"If it meant keeping them safe," my voice is unwavering as I stare him down. "I refuse to raise a human baby in this life."

"This life?" He shakes his head. "And a human? We don't even know—"

"The doctor said there's a 50/50 chance," I interrupt, nervously wringing my hands, "I'm useless here and I'm a full grown adult. I don't want to think about what would happen if we stay here and the baby is a human. If it turns out they're a shifter, I'll give them the choice to come back here."

There's a beat of silence, and I hope that he's viewing my admission for what it is: a compromise. If the baby isn't human, I'll give them the choice to come back and stay. I would be out of my depth raising a shifter by myself anyway. Hopefully, they would choose to come back, but I'd have to cross that bridge when I got to it.

"You can't tell me you're still thinking about leaving?" he asks incredulously.

"I'm not just thinking about it, I'm leaving," I say with finality.

"You're just deciding?" His voice is incredulous. "You're not even going to try to talk to me about this? To find a solution that doesn't involve ripping our family apart, possibly destroying the pack and breaking my heart?"

My words falter, but I shake my head. I can't let his words affect me. I have to be strong. I have to think of my baby. "Yes. I'm just deciding." Swallowing, I look at him pleadingly. "Please, Elijah. This is what's best—"

"The hell it is," his voice raises, "you're not taking my baby from me, Lucy."

"Is your pride worth more to you than the safety of your child?"

"A child, human or not, needs their father."

"You can't make me—"

"I fucking can, and I will. I'll force the fucking mate bond on you if I have to!" His face is screwed up in anger, and his hands are in fists at his side.

My heart stutters at his words, and ice fills my veins. "If you do that," I breathe heavily, "you would be no different than Leon, and I would *never* forgive you for that."

"I—" He stops, his face paling as the impact of my words seems to hit him. "You're right," he murmurs, his gaze searching mine before he abruptly turns on his heels, leaving me alone in my room.

The second I'm alone, tears spill down my face. My heart shatters for having hurt him. I don't want to hurt him. Hell, I don't want to leave him, but after everything—do I really have any other choice?

From the moment I met Elijah, I was only ever given one chance at having my own say in how my life would go. And that was when I found him on my front porch. If I'd left him there... none of this would have ever happened.

But fate be damned...this is where I stand now.

My heart, falling to pieces, as I try to understand what to do next.

Chapter 22

Alpha's Orders

Lucy

Despite the fight between us yesterday, my heart has lifted slightly. My mind is still mixed with confusion, but something deep inside me makes me second guess myself. A drive within my heart that tells me to wait...that tells me not to make any hasty decisions just yet. Pulling my jacket around me, I plan for a walk in the cool air to help clear my mind. But the moment I open my bedroom door, I met the hard stare of Riftan.

"Riftan, what are you doing here?" I ask, brows knitting together in confusion.

A heavy sigh escapes me, as he shakes his head. "Guard duty."

"Guard duty? Why here? I was just getting ready to take a walk."

He hesitates for a moment, before shaking his head again. "I'm afraid I can't let you do that."

"Excuse me?"

"It's not my choice. You're not allowed to leave your room without permission," he replies, my eyes widening slightly as fury fills me. I'm not surprised after the conversation Elijah and I had yesterday, but instead of trying to speak to me again, he pulls this shit.

"Sorry, Lucy. Alpha's orders," he replies once more, smiling apologetically.

"*What* were the *full* Alpha's orders?" I ask, trying to control the anger seething beneath my skin.

"He's said that you're not to leave the pack house, at least not until you're less of a..." He trails off, almost like he's unsure of whether or not he should finish his sentence.

"Less of a *what*?"

"Flight risk." He winces, as if bracing himself for me to lash out at him.

All that escapes me is a gentle nod before I make my way back into my room and remove my jacket as I close the door. Once again, pacing like a caged animal trying to think through everything that has happened. Only stopping every once in a while to deeply breathe through a wave of nausea. I don't know if it's the hormones or what, but I'm even more pissed about this than I was when Elijah took me from my father's cabin.

A few hours later, and I've spent the day stewing in my own anger, waiting for Elijah to try to show his face so I can give him a piece of my mind. It's almost dinner time when a light knock on the door has me on edge. Raring to go, I wrench my door open aggressively. Expecting to see Elijah.

"Fuck off—" I stop when I see Bailey in my doorway. "Bailey." I grimace, backing away from the door before turning to sit upon the bed. "To what do I owe the pleasure?" My voice is as dry as I can make it.

"Lucy..." she starts, then sighs and shakes her head, moving to sit across from me on the bed, tucking one foot underneath her.

"I'm assuming fuckface has told you?" I ask quietly, drawing my knees up to my chest, wincing at the way my skin tightens around my scars.

"If by 'fuckface', you mean my brother, then yes. He told me yesterday. Why..." She visibly swallows. "Why would you try to leave, Lucy?"

"There's a chance the baby could be human. Completely defenseless in the world of your people. What kind of mother would I be if I raised a human baby in this environment?"

She starts to shake her head, "You don't *know* it'll be a—"

"Don't even start with me, Bailey," I bite out. "I've already had this conversation once. This is all you guys do. When you don't like a decision I make, you make me do it your way. I'm done." Throwing up my hands, I walk to the door. "When I'm not being thrown over a wolf's shoulder and dragged to somewhere I don't want to be, I'm being locked in my room. I'm not going to pretend to be happy about it. "

Her face is sad, and she reaches a hand out toward me. "Lucy..."

"No." Shaking my head, I hold the door open. "Never once have *any* of you stopped to ask me what *I* want or even how *I* truly feel. You're trying to change me without any consideration into my opinion of things. I'm not going to let you guys do that to my child as well. Now, please...leave. I want to be alone."

"You know," Bailey says, making her way towards the door. "You say that, Lucy, but at the same time you were planning to take my brother's child away without asking him how he felt either."

She isn't wrong. I'm stopped in my tracks, processing my thoughts as tears brim my eyes. Was I a horrible person for wanting to take my mate's child away? Yeah, probably. But it wasn't to be cruel. I want to leave to protect our child.

"You're not wrong, Bailey," I finally admit. My tear filled gaze meets hers. "But there's a difference. I knew that if I tried to talk to him, he wouldn't listen. Because he never *truly* listens. And even after I told him, instead of asking me why I felt I had to do that or even trying to listen to me, he decided to make me a prisoner instead. What's the point anymore? Of any of this..."

Opening and closing her mouth, she stares at me. Speechless

over the truth I shared with her. Elijah and I are both in the wrong, but at least I'm thinking of someone else besides myself. I could stay here and be a prisoner if he wanted me to be.

But our child shouldn't be, and the safety of my child is the only thing that matters.

Two days later, I'm hunched over the toilet, retching my guts out. Elijah did come to see me that night after Bailey left, but I refused to let him in. He still attempts to see me every single day, but I refuse to give in.

This is the first time I've actually had to throw up since getting pregnant, and it's thoroughly kicking my ass. I snuck downstairs to grab my dinner as usual, and locked my door behind me. My punishment lifted to only not leaving the packhouse now—not that it's any better.

I was only three bites into my grilled cheese when it hit me full force and I barely made it to the bathroom in time. Sitting back and wiping my mouth, I rest my head against the cool tile, praying for reprieve. After a moment, my stomach settles. Thinking that I'm done, I move to stand, only to be overtaken by another wave of nausea, which promptly puts me on my knees again. I don't think I've even eaten as much as what's coming out of me. Suddenly, there's a loud crashing sound that I can't investigate because again, I'm throwing up.

Footsteps quicken to the bathroom, and I feel a refreshingly cool hand on my forehead. "It's okay, baby, I've got you," Elijah murmurs to me as he gathers my hair, holding it back for me as I retch again.

"You better not have broke the fucking door—" I can hardly speak my stomach is revolting against me, and he chuckles softly while rubbing soothing circles across my back.

"I'll replace it," he says, and slowly, my stomach stops trying to turn itself inside out. I breathe for a moment, turning my head to the side and focusing on the tiled wall next to me. Focusing on the feel of Elijah's hand on my back, my eyes drift shut as I fall into an exhausted sleep.

When my eyes crack open, I'm back in my bed. I vaguely recall Elijah gently carrying me and tucking me in. Sitting up on my elbows, I wince at the sight of my bedroom door hanging off its hinges. Elijah really helped me last night. If he hadn't, I'd probably still be passed out on the bathroom floor.

Glancing at my bedside table, I see a tray with some saltine crackers, some ginger ale, and a stack of my favorite books. A small smile finds its way to my face when I pick up the book on the top of the stack, one that I specifically told Eli that I could read over and over and never grow bored of. I have a signed copy in the box of books that I left with my neighbor when I came here. Sighing, I open the front cover, and see this one's signed as well. My eyes scan over the message, "To Lucy".

My heart stops.

This is my book.

How did he get my book?

I pick up the other books and look for my stamp—the one that my grandparents got me for Christmas one year with the wording, "Property of the Lucy McIntire Library" on the inside cover. All of them have it.

He got *all* my books.

This is a bribe. It has to be. Why else would he go through all this trouble? But...it's only been a few days since everything happened, I don't think he would have been able to get everything here that quickly.

The sound of footsteps shuffling has me lifting my head again. Elijah is standing in my doorway, holding a whole ass door. "Sorry, I didn't think you'd be awake yet," he says, kneeling to undo the pins in the hinges of the broken door. "You can just ignore me."

"You found an entire door pretty quickly," I smirk, and he chuckles.

"Ripping doors off their hinges isn't as uncommon of an occurrence as you might think. I learned the hard way and ordered these in bulk." He works, pulling the pins out, his eyes darting over to me periodically. There's nothing but concern in his eyes for me when he looks at me, and I wonder if maybe I reacted too harshly to this whole situation.

"Can...can we talk?" I swallow, watching as he finishes fastening the new door on the hinges. Nodding, he comes to sit on the bed with me. He doesn't say anything as I nibble on a cracker eyeing the books next to me. "You...you got my books." I don't know what I'm hoping to confirm here. Maybe I'm hoping he isn't trying to bribe me into staying here.

"I meant to..." He rubs the back of his neck. "I've been looking for them since you mentioned you had to leave them with your neighbor, it wasn't a bribe or anything, I swear."

My brow furrows. "I mentioned that weeks ago."

"Yeah. I sent one of my guys to collect them from your old neighbor, but I guess she wanted to make some quick cash and sold the box to a secondhand bookstore, and then a collector picked them all up. It took a while but we finally tracked them all down."

She sold my books! I fucking knew it.

As angry as I am that my shitty neighbor sold my books, my heart fills with joy that he found them. "Thank you. I can't tell you how much this means to me. Where are the others?"

"The box is in my office, I'll bring it by later." He grins. "But, I have a feeling that's not really what you want to talk about."

"It's not," I admit, looking down. "Look, I know I haven't outright said it yet, but I do love you." A sigh escapes me, and Elijah squeezes my hand, letting me know it's alright to keep going. "But...this wasn't my choice. None of it. Not really. I just... if the baby is a shifter, I want the baby to have a choice. The Moon Goddess took away my choice in all of this, and I don't want to do that to the baby. Especially when I know what it's like to be the weak one among the wolves."

His brow furrows and his tone is puzzled. "Weak? Why would they be weak?"

"Because their mother is human." I shrug. "I mean, I would assume that my blood would dilute any power they would have, even if they are a shifter."

Elijah shakes his head. "I've been researching the last couple of days. Lucy, all but five of the couples researched were chosen mates, not fated. In the cases of chosen mates, the children who were human still had the strength and speed close to a wolf shifter in human form, and the biological shifters were the same, the only difference is they could shift forms." He grips my hand tight. "But the fated mates? There were only five, but one was human and four wolf shifters. The human had speed and strength equal to that of a regular shifter, and of the two shifters that had Alpha blood, they were just as strong, if not stronger than their wolf shifter parent."

Tears sting my eyes at his admission. "So…even if they're human, they won't be too weak to thrive here?"

"No." He smiles, tears in his eyes as well. "No matter what, they should be just as strong as any other wolf shifter, even if they're human."

"Oh, Elijah." I lean into him, crying into his chest. I didn't realize how heavily the entire situation had been weighing on me until it was lifted. That had been my biggest concern since I found out I was pregnant. The doctor hadn't explained any of that, and I'd assumed he was more familiar with it all considering he works for the packs, but I guess not.

He wraps his arms around me, tucking my head under his chin, rubbing my back with his hands.

"I'm so sorry." I gasp through my tears. "I was going to leave with your baby, and I didn't even do proper research!" The last part of my sentence comes out as a wail, and I don't miss the fact that Elijah's chest is shaking as he holds in a laugh.

I know I'm being hysterical, and that it's probably just the hormones, but I can't stop myself from crying harder into him. "It's not funny," I cry, but there's still a faint hint of humor laced in his voice.

"I know it's not. I know. But, baby, you're going to give me whiplash from how fast you go from zero to sixty."

A laugh escapes me despite my tears, and I pull away from him, wiping my eyes. Taking a few deep breaths, I attempt to calm my hammering heart. "I am sorry," I say, sniffling. "I love you. I do, so very much. And I don't care if it's because of the mate bond, or because you take care of me, or because you had someone track down my books, but I do." I swallow, nodding. "I love you, Elijah."

He leans over, planting a sweet, gentle, kiss on my lips. "I love you too, my sweet Lucy."

"More like Crazy Lucy," I mutter, and he bursts out laughing, the sound of it filling my stomach with butterflies. I hadn't realized how long it has been since I heard him laugh. "And I'm not going anywhere," I add, pecking him on the lips. "No matter how much you beg me."

"Oh, Lu," he says leaning back on the bed and patting his chest. "I'll never beg you to go anywhere." He sighs in contentment as I nestle into his side, my head on his chest, and my arm around his waist. He strokes lazily up and down my arm, and for the first time since coming here, I truly feel like I'm home, right where I need to be.

Chapter 23

Surprise

Lucy

Things are going better. It's been a few days since I replaced the door that I ripped off its hinges to get to Lucy, and she's acting more like herself again. Once I had Doctor Sullivan come in and reiterate what I told her about the research on human-wolf shifter interbreeding, she visibly relaxed and she seems a lot happier now.

While he was here, he brought in a medicinal cocktail that acts as an anti-nausea medication and as long as she takes it every day before she goes to bed, she seems to feel much better during the day.

I should probably still be mad at her for trying to leave with the baby, but really, it's just a testament to what an amazing mother she's going to be. With what limited information she had, she was making what she thought was the best choice for the baby and I can't really fault her for that. I can only thank the Moon Goddess that my dad had some weird interests and had a book onhand about the subject.

"Hey, Lu?" I knock lightly on her door, cracking it open. She's lounging on her bed, reading one of her fathers journals again. My heart clenches at the fact that she'll never know him. Even though Lucy is barely seven weeks along now, I can't imagine just abandoning my kid for any reason. I'd been looking into why her father came to work for the pack in the first place, and all I could find in my dad's records was that he was a researcher that was sometimes called up to pack territory to tend to minor injuries.

I want to tell Lucy what I know…but things have just sort of settled again after she was taken. I'll wait until I have some more information before I tell her anything.

"Hey." She looks up at me, smiling, and my heart flutters in my chest. Her soft, brown hair falls around her face in waves, and her beautiful green eyes stare expectantly at me. She's in leggings that show off her perfectly round ass, and an adorably comfy looking sweater.

"How are you and Pup doing?" That's what we've taken to calling the baby, 'Pup'.

"We're good." She grins, her hand running over her lower stomach. "Come lay with me?"

Internally, I groan. I want to go to her so badly, but I have to show her what I've been working on for her. "You have no idea how badly I want to," I say, leaning on the doorframe, "but, I have a feeling you'll have other plans once you see my surprise for you."

"Surprise?" Her eyes light up, and she scrambles off the bed to get to me, taking my hand. "Lead the way." She motions out the door and I chuckle, pulling her into the hallway. We go down a ways, past my office, and she looks around. "We're not…we're not going downstairs?"

"The surprise isn't downstairs," I inform her, and take her to the end of the hall, in front of a lone door. She moves in front of me, dropping my hand.

"I've never noticed this door before…" she murmurs, running her hands along the carved images on the door. Wolves, and books, and images of different desserts decorate the door, and her voice is quiet as she looks at me. "Elijah…what is this?"

I lean forward, my mouth brushing against the shell of her ear. "Why don't you go in and see?" I lean around her, grasping the doorknob, and push the door open.

The gasp that leaves her mouth as she steps into the room is nothing short of magical. Her steps are slow, like she's afraid it's all an illusion and if she moves too fast, everything will disappear. "Is this...mine?" She turns to me, her eyes watering.

I nod, a small grin finding its way to my lips. "Yes, Lucy. It's all yours."

She whirls, running her hands along the books that line the bookshelves in the room. I tried to get it as close to an actual library as I could, the way the shelves are set up create small alcoves set up with comfortable chairs and little lamps for reading. There's a desk in the corner of the room, and a fireplace. It's big enough to be a small library, it takes up half the third floor.

I've spent the last two weeks having this room curated just for her. "You won't be disturbed here," I say quietly, trailing her. "Unless you want to be. But you'll have space to do whatever you want. Writing your book, or just reading—" She whirls to face me, her eyes shining.

"What was this room before? Why have I never seen it?" Her brows are furrowed, like she's worried about something.

"It was my bedroom." I tuck a piece of hair behind her ear. "But I thought...maybe I could just move in with you?" Her brow furrows and I quickly say, "unless you're not ready. I'm more than willing to sleep on the couch in my office until you are."

She shakes her head, grabbing the front of my shirt with both her hands. "I would like that...I just, I feel so bad that you gave up your space for me."

"I'd rather be with you." I give her a gentle smile, as she pulls me down by my shirt to meet my lips in a kiss.

"You haven't even seen the best part," I murmur as she breaks the kiss, taking her hand, leading her to the part of the room with the desk in the corner. The view was blocked by a bookshelf, but as we round the corner, a tiny gasp leaves her.

"These are all your favorites...Lucy McIntyre Library originals." I grin, motioning to the standalone shelf that sits right next to the most plush chair and footrest I could find.

"That's why you never brought me my box of books." She raises an eyebrow at me, and I chuckle.

"Yes, this is why. There's a small table for whatever treat you've made or some hot cocoa..." Then I lead her over to the desk. "I've managed to get my hands on a laptop, and it has the word processor software installed already." I elbow her gently and she rolls her eyes at me. "I just...I don't want you to regret staying here."

Shaking her head, she steps up to me, wrapping her arms around my neck, and pulls me in for a passionate kiss. I let her take the lead, thankful that I can feel all of her raw emotions she pulls back, and says against my mouth. "I could never regret staying here with you." She dives back into my mouth, and I meet her, greedily taking what she's offering. Sliding my tongue across her lips, she groans as she parts them, allowing me entry. She's fucking intoxicating.

My wolf whines at me in the back of my mind.

Quickly, I reach down, grasping the back of her thighs, and lift her so our chests are pressed together. Kneading her perfect ass in my hands, I set her down on the desk, breaking our kiss. Her eyes are still closed, and she's frozen for a moment before opening her eyes, "What are you—"

"It's hard for me..." I clear my throat. "It's hard for me to give you a space that I'm not a part of. I want all of you, all of the time, but I know that you need your own space as well." She nods, and I continue, "I think I know how to remedy that."

She parts her lips for me as I lean back down to kiss her, taking my time, my hand on her cheek. Our tongues dance lazily together as my hand moves down her neck, past her collarbone, massaging the perfect mound of her breast. She moans into my mouth, they must be extra sensitive because of the pregnancy.

I don't stop there, though, I keep my mouth on hers, nipping at her, teasing, as I work my hand down her front, kneading her clothed pussy with the heel of my hand. A whimper escapes her as I continue to work, moving in slow circles.

"Elijah, please—" she gasps as I slip my hand down the front of her leggings, my fingers running through the soaked folds of her pussy.

"So wet for me already," I growl, and the front of my pants strain against my hard cock. Ignoring the pressure, I delve a finger into her, pumping in and out as her gasps grow louder against my mouth. She's lifting her hips to meet my fingers, my chest rumbles in approval as I slip a second finger into her. She throws her head back, a moan escaping her lips, and I move down to her neck, licking, nipping and tasting her as she rides my hand.

Without warning, I withdraw, and she protests, but is quickly silenced when I gently push her shoulders down, causing her to lay with her back on the desk, her head falling over the side. Peeling off the leggings, I grab her ankles, and place hot, open mouthed kisses along the insides of her legs, until I get to her soaked, aching center. She groans, and attempts to push her pussy into my face, "Tsk, tsk, my love." I playfully nip at the inside of her thigh, causing her to cry out. "Patience."

I tease her for a moment longer before finally running my tongue all the way up her slit, earning a guttural moan from her. "You taste so sweet," I murmur against her folds, and continue working her, licking up and down her sensitive bundle of nerves. Her hands tangle in hair as I nip and suck at her, and when I put my finger back into her, she loses it. She grips my hair tighter, my scalp burning deliciously, and she bucks against my face as I bury my mouth into her.

I growl in encouragement, which only spurs her to ride my mouth faster. Her body starts to contract around my fingers, and I can hear her breathing growing more and more ragged. Her cries reach a crescendo as the pulsating around my fingers come to a peak, and I can *feel* the orgasm hit her, her walls contracting around my fingers as her sweetness fills my mouth. Her thrusting slows, and her hand falls out of my hair. Lifting my head, I grin like a madman at the sight of her sprawled out on the desk, limp with satisfaction.

Licking my lips, I move to help her up, and she slides off the desk. Instead of moving to pull her pants back on though, she peels off her shirt and bra, turns around, and bends over the desk, giving me an unfettered view of her wet, glistening pussy. "I want you inside me," she breathes, wiggling her hips enticingly.

"Fuck, Lucy," I groan, pulling off my shirt and unbuckling my pants. "I was ready to walk out of here, blue balls and everything, and you just have to go and say things like that." She whimpers in response, and pulling out my dick, I pump it a few times, spreading around the precum that's already beaded at my tip. My hands grasp her hips, as she tilts herself up to meet me as my cock slides perfectly into her hot, wet pussy.

A moan escapes her as she presses her face into the desk, and I pull out almost all the way, only to slam back into her until my balls hit her clit. A sharp cry escapes her as her nails struggle for purchase on the smooth surface of the desk.

"Hold on to the end of the desk," I grunt, pulling out again, and she does, right as I fill her once again. My thrusts are measured, controlled. Her breaths are labored, and a small cry escapes her each time I bottom out, my thighs slapping against the back of her.

"Elijah." She's breathless, and she tilts her head to look at me. "I want you to lose control. Don't hold back."

Fuck.

Something in her words unleashes the feral side of me, and I hunch over her, my movements becoming more erratic. Wrapping both arms around her body, I use one hand to rub her clit, and the other palm her breast. Her small cries become loud and uninhibited as she calls my name.

There's no sound in the library but the slapping of our bodies coming together, her screams, and my moans.

"Fuck, fuck, fuck, Elijah!" she cries as her walls contract

around my cock, the sensation pushing me over the edge to my own release, and a strangled gasp escapes me as I empty myself into her. I ride the wave of both of our orgasms, slowing to a stop, and breathing hard. Kissing her back, I pull out, and hand her a few tissues from the tissue box on the desk.

As she cleans up and we both get dressed, I wrap my arms around her again, pulling her in for a kiss that I hope conveys just how much she means to me. Then I whisper mischievously, "now you'll have to think of me every single time you use this desk."

She huffs a laugh and playfully hits my arm, but I see her smile as she picks out a book from the shelves with her personal books, and flops comfily into the chair. Planting a kiss on her head, I relish the sight of her smiling to herself as she opens her book, and I slip out the door, leaving her in the peace I promised her.

Chapter 24

Back to the Drawing Board

Lucy

The last four weeks have gone by in a blur, and I've never been happier that I decided to stay with the pack. My hand travels over the slight swell of my belly, and a rush of warmth overtakes at the thought of my little pup growing inside my womb.

Doctor Sullivan says that typically, werewolf women are pregnant for 30 weeks before the babies are ready, and it varies from couple to couple on the human-werewolf spectrum. If Doctor Sullivan is to be believed, the ones with Alpha blood are more typical of a regular werewolf pregnancy.

If the size of my growing baby bump is any indication, I'd say he's right. I haven't felt them move yet, but Doc says it'll be soon, and if we travel to the hospital, he can tell us if the baby will be a boy or a girl. I think I want to find out. There's another small bedroom on the third floor of the pack house that I want to turn into a nursery, and I want to be able to start decorating.

My boots shuffle in the snow; it's starting to get a little warmer and the snow is not as deep as it usually is. I'm on my daily walk, which I've read is good for me and the baby. Members of the pack wave to me and call out, asking how the baby is doing.

Every other day, Silvy runs up to me with a craft or a picture or something else that she made for the baby, and I always thank her, tucking it into my jacket. I know she won't come find me today though, because yesterday she brought me a necklace made with dried macaroni and string.

Instead, Elijah's mom finds me today. She's been scarce the last few months, apparently trying to give me space to settle into my role. I told her she didn't have to do that, but then she said that her deceased mother-in-law was so overbearing and condescending, she decided she would never be that way to any daughter-in-law she had.

"Lucy." She smiles, coming up to me with a bag on her arm from the general store. "How are you feeling?"

"Hi Sage," I greet. "I'm doing well. The baby is growing normally, according to Doctor Sullivan."

"That's good." She looks me over, as if assessing me herself for any health concerns. "I was about to come see you at the pack house. Just to visit." She smiles again, seemingly finding nothing of concern to dote on me about.

"I'm on my walk now, but I should be back in 30 minutes," I tell her, rubbing my hand absentmindedly over my belly.

"Don't trouble yourself, dear." She smiles kindly. "I'll come by a different time, I have some things to do." Her eyes trail to my belly. "May I?" she asks, holding out a hand.

Grinning, I nod, and she gently presses her hand to the swell of my belly. "Hello, dear, it's me, Mamaw." I raise a brow and she chuckles. "You're right, that doesn't sound right. I'm still trying to figure out what I want to be called."

"Back to the drawing board?" I chuckle, and she laughs as well.

"Maybe I'll try Mimi. Or Gran Gran. Or…"

"Grandma?" I tease, and she pats my shoulder.

"We'll see." Her eyes glint mischievously as she walks away, back towards her home among the individual houses.

I resume my journey, following the path I take every day. I'm winded coming up the hill, which is my life now, and I smile as I look over the pond that Elijah and I go ice skating on now and again.

We haven't gone in the last couple of weeks, but I'm not sure how I could do it now anyway, with the way my body gets so tired. He's had more time to spend with me since he re-evaluated the way patrols are done, and we spend most of our time reading together, or playing board games. I'm teaching him some of my moms recipes, and last night we stayed up late as he watched me make macarons—the way he should have had them the night I ran back to the cabin before I was kidnapped.

My libido has gone through the roof the last couple of weeks as well, and I find myself more desperate for his touch than ever. I don't know if it's the mate bond or what but he seems just as desperate for me. I blush at the memory of sucking him off behind the kitchen island while the macarons cooled last night, his hands tangled in my hair until his hot release hit the back of my throat. Anyone could have walked in, and somehow that just added to the thrill of it.

Poor Riftan was subject to a full on show, walking into Elijah's office on a Tuesday afternoon, only to see Elijah smack my ass as I was bent over his desk, taking me from behind. Riftan's face turned almost as red as his hair as he sputtered an apology and left, the door slamming shut behind him. Elijah only left me to lock the door, then came back, reinserting himself and grasping the back of my neck to pull me up for a hard, desperate kiss.

Apparently fucking on desks is our thing now.

I'm jolted out of my memories by the sound of footsteps. I think they're coming from the other side of the pond. They grow louder, and I do a double take when I see Thallia with her head down, coming toward me from the other side of the pond.

"Thallia?" I call out, and she startles when she hears me, whipping her head in my direction. She looks like shit. Her normally perfect and fluffy hair is dull and lifeless. Her eyes have dark circles underneath them and her skin is pale. She comes up the hill and stops next to me, her eyes narrowed.

"Are you okay?" I ask sincerely. "Have you been sleeping?"

"I'm fine." She brushes me off. "I'm doing better than you anyway."

My eyebrows shoot up. "Better than me?"

This bitch.

She's on the defensive. Her shoulders are hunched, and she's not looking directly at me. Come on, I know she was rejected by my mate, but damn. Her audacity is astounding.

"Yeah, I'm not the one who was kidnapped and tortured," she sneers, her eyes darting to my legs.

I swallow.

Nobody was supposed to know about that. Did Elijah...?

No, he wouldn't do that.

Her gaze lingers on my legs for a moment, and my scars feel like they're on fire under the heat of her gaze.

"What do you—" Before I can get my question out, she quickly harrumphs, moving swiftly past me toward the pack general store. I know that Elijah moved her to a different house to keep her away from us, but would I have to change my daily walk too?

It doesn't sit right with me that she knows about my legs or that I was tortured. Only Elijah, Riftan, and I know what really happened. So unless one of the guys told her...no. Shaking my head, I know that they wouldn't do that. So that just leaves...my heart drops in my chest. It couldn't be true, could it? I go back to the pack house, not stopping until I'm opening the door to Elijah's office.

"Lucy?" He looks up from whatever he was working on. I must have some sort of look on my face because he immediately asks, "are you okay?"

"I...I don't know," I admit, walking into the office. I can't bring myself to sit, so I just stand next to the chair on the other side of his desk.

"Is it the baby?" he asks, his brows knit together.

"No, I..." I'm unsure of how to broach the subject without having a repeat of last time. He has to believe me, right? "I think..." I swallow, forcing the words out, as I start to pace the room. "I think that Thallia was working with Alpha Leon."

I wait for him to refute me. For him to tell me I'm being crazy. But he just asks, "what makes you say that?"

"I ran into her on my walk. She...she doesn't look good, Eli. Like she hasn't slept in weeks. And she...she knew about my legs. The torture. So unless you or Riftan said anything to her..."

"Never," he adamantly shakes his head.

"I didn't think so," I admit, then wrap my arms around myself. "She looked at me like she hates me. I don't know if it's just because she's still in love with you or there's something else going on, but I really don't think we can trust her. At first it was like we just couldn't trust her to keep her hands to herself, but now I don't think we can trust her to not put the pack in danger." I grip my arms tighter. "I...I'm worried about the baby with her around."

He nods at my words, running a hand over his face. "I don't want to believe it, but what's that saying? When someone shows you over and over again who they are...believe them." He shakes his head. "Either way, we obviously can't trust her. Even if she wasn't working with Leon, the fact that she would even say anything about it to you is...unsettling." He leans back in his chair. "I'll have Riftan keep an eye on her, and have him assign someone from the warriors to keep close track of her comings and goings." He looks at me, regret in his eyes. "I'm sorry, Lucy, that must have been really unsettling. Riftan will make sure she can't approach you again."

Swallowing, I walk around to the other side of the desk, letting Elijah wrap his arms around my middle, pressing his face into my belly. One of his hands caresses the side of my baby bump, and my heart swells with a love I never knew was possible. There's a slight flutter deep in my belly that makes me gasp.

"What?" He jumps back, looking at me with concerned eyes.

"I think I felt the baby move." I smile, grabbing his hand and placing it back on my belly. There it is again. "That's your daddy," I whisper to the life growing inside me as Elijah looks at me with adoration. "Do you feel him? He loves you so much."

"You can feel Pup moving?" His eyes are wide as he moves his hand across my belly, and I nod, tears welling up in my eyes.

When I found out I was pregnant, I was so worried. I thought my life was over, and I couldn't believe I was so stupid to let myself get knocked up. But sitting here with Elijah, our little family huddled together, I realize I couldn't have been more wrong. This little life growing inside me will be the greatest blessing the Moon Goddess could have ever given me. I guess I'm slightly less of an atheist now.

"I love you, Elijah." My voice is hoarse as I lean down to kiss him gently. I'll let him fuck me senseless later, but right now, my heart just wants the tender love and affection he's so good at giving me.

He pulls back from the kiss. "And I love you, Lucy." He wipes a tear from my eyes, and kisses my tears away. "Nobody will ever hurt you again," he promises me, and against all reasonable expectations, I believe him. This baby could not have been luckier, being born a child to a man like Elijah.

After he's sure I'm not going to keep crying, he rests his face against my belly again and talks to the baby. "Your mommy loves you so much. She would do anything to keep you safe. She is the most amazing, strongest, most resilient person I know."

Chapter 25

Chocolate Chip Cookies

Lucy

"Do you want some dessert?" My voice is low in his ear, and I feel his chest rumble in approval as he tightens his arms around me. The last few days since my run in with Thallia have passed without incident, and tonight, I had come into his office to let him know I was craving chocolate chip cookies. I hadn't been at his side for more than two seconds before he pulled me into his lap, content to keep working on whatever he was doing despite my presence.

That is, until I mentioned dessert.

"I could lay you on my desk right now and have some dessert." The heat in his voice makes it hard to resist, and my pussy clenches at his words, but I *really* want those cookies.

"Behave." I suppress a giggle, disentangling myself from him, and standing next to his chair. "I meant literal dessert, you sex-crazed wolf."

"Oh?" He arches a brow, leaning back. "It didn't seem like *I* was the sex-crazed one when you were wiggling your ass in the air this morning, begging me for my—"

"Anyway." I shoot him what I can only hope is a death glare, earning an arrogant smirk from him, before I continue sweetly, "I'm really desperate for some chocolate chip cookies, and I'll make enough for you if you ask me very, *very* nicely."

"Please." He stands, leaning down and capturing my lips in a kiss. His hands are on my hips, and a gasp escapes me when he gently captures my bottom lip with his teeth. He releases me with a growl that has me thinking he was on the right track with his first mention of *dessert*.

Cookies, Lucy. Think of the cookies.

Shaking my head, I back away from him, smiling. "You're a bad boy, Elijah." I raise a brow. "Maybe you won't be getting any cookies after all."

"You love me." He grins, sitting back down at his desk.

"I do." I breathe, my hand on the doorknob. His look of love and adoration fills my heart to the brim.

Fine, I'll make him the fucking cookies.

Right before my steps take me out of the room, the lights in his office and hallway flicker. Glancing at him, I take his vaguely concerned expression. "I'll have Laurent take a look at the wiring of the building tomorrow."

"Laurent does...wiring?"

"Electrical engineering," he clarifies, going back to his work.

Nodding as I process that random tidbit of information, as I head down to the kitchen. I wonder how many wolves are like Laurent—how many have careers and dreams and training outside of being in the pack. Suddenly, I find myself wanting to ask about everyone's passions.

Maybe I could start a book club.

Or a little artist's corner.

I'm itching to get to know everyone not just as members of the pack...but *people*.

A feeling of calm comes over me as I enter the kitchen. As usual, it's empty this time of night and everyone's retired to their beds. Silence as I work in the kitchen is something that soothes me, and it's not something that happens often unless I creep down here at 11:30 pm like I'm doing now.

Humming to myself as I mix my flour, baking soda, cornstarch, and salt together, I curse to myself as I realize that I didn't get out a second bowl for my wet ingredients. Muttering to myself, I'm looking through one of the kitchen cabinets when the lights flicker again. My eyes run over the ceiling lights suspiciously, as I pull out my second bowl, daring them to give out on me and keep me from making the chocolate chip cookies I'm craving.

When they don't go out again, I place my second bowl on the island, move to the fridge, and pull out the eggs and butter. The lights go out before I make it back to the counter.

Shit. It's pitch black in here.

Here's to hoping my internal compass works well enough that I can make it back to the island without dropping anything on the floor. Before I can take a step, though, the back kitchen door creaks open, and quiet footsteps sound behind me.

"Hey," I call out, hoping to get this situation sorted out. "Do you know what's going on with the lights? I can't *see* anything—"

A hand covers my mouth from behind, muffling my screams as another hand wraps around my body, pinning my arms to my side. My milk and eggs drop out my hands and crash to the floor, creating a mess with loud thump. Bucking against the body of the attacker, they hardly move a muscle as I fight against them with everything I have for them to loosen their grip.

But they don't.

I have to make noise. I have to draw attention because nobody knows what's going on down here. Pressing my body back against my attacker, I flail my legs out, managing to knock the metal mixing bowl off the table with a clang, and the body behind me tenses, but doesn't let up as they start to drag me back towards the kitchen door.

I was going to be taken again.

No.

No, I wouldn't do it again.

The scars on my legs sear with a phantom heat. I will not relive that torture.

My baby. They would not put my baby in danger.

Maybe it's the adrenaline, or maybe it's my baby lending me some werewolf strength, or maybe it's just pure dumb luck, but I manage to wrench an arm free from my attacker's hold, and jam my elbow back as hard as I can into the soft pit of their stomach.

With a gasp, the attacker lets their hand go slack on my mouth, and I draw my breath, releasing it in an ear piercing scream. "Elijah!"

Immediately, I hear footsteps upstairs, and my attacker grasps my arms roughly, hissing, "human bitch." in my ear before roughly shoving me forward, knocking the wind from me when my stomach collides with the island.

That voice. If I didn't know any better, I'd say that was...

"Lucy!" Elijah roared, his footsteps pounding on the steps, the sound of people bumping into the staircase walls an indication that he was determined to get to me first, no matter what.

"Lucy!" Though I can't see his face in this dark, I feel the gentle caress of his hand against my cheek. "What happened, baby? Are you okay? Who made this mess?"

"You can see the mess?" I choke out, still out of my element in complete darkness.

"Shifter vision." His voice brushes me off, before his hands grasp my shoulders. "What happened, Lucy?"

"I was making my cookies when the power went out, and I was attacked." Murmurs went through the crowd, and based on the volume, I'd wager I had every single warrior in the pack house in my kitchen right now.

"Riftan," Elijah barks in Alpha mode, "Go outside and see what you can find. They must have fled out the back door after Lucy screamed."

"On it, Alpha." Riftan's voice sounds, followed by the sound of the kitchen door opening and closing again.

"Then what happened?" His voice is soothing me, one hand

working its way back up to my face to rub gentle circles on my cheek.

"They tried to take me out the back door. I wouldn't let them take me again, Elijah." My voice grows hysterical as I try to keep the tears from spilling over. "I can't let them hurt me or the baby."

"I know, baby, I know." He wraps his arms around me, and I sink into his embrace, "Do you have any idea who it could have been?"

"I think." Swallowing, I focus on the memory of the voice I heard. It was her, I know it. "I think it was Thallia."

Murmurs erupted around the kitchen again. From what I can gather, nobody is shocked that she had the capacity to attack me, just that she dared to do it under Elijah's roof.

Elijah stiffens around me. "This is my fault," he whispers, and I feel his forehead pressed against mine.

Suddenly, the lights come on, and Laurent comes in through the back door. "The breaker was switched off for the kitchen and staircase only." He nods to Elijah. "It seems like this was a very targeted attack on our future Luna."

He grits his teeth, the vein in his neck threatening to pop out before Riftan comes back in. "I couldn't find anyone. I followed some footprints down the skating pond, but then they disappeared."

"Go check out Thallia's house. With any luck, she has the good sense to run away. If she hasn't, bring her here. Danger to my mate and child will not be tolerated."

The warriors murmur in agreement, and I can see the indignation on their faces. They care about me. As much as I'm shaken up by this attack, it warms my heart to see that I'm accepted here.

By all but one, apparently.

Once everyone files back up to their rooms, leaving just me, Elijah, and Laurent, in the kitchen, I'm able to see the full extent of the mess the attack left me with. There's flour everywhere, eggs cracked on the floor, and a puddle of milking slowly seeping its way under the fridge. Elijah and Laurent are talking in low voices about setting up a security system, and before I can help it, tears are rolling off my cheeks and onto the floor.

This is so, so, stupid. I can't believe I'm crying about this.

I feel warm hands on my arms and look to see Bailey's frown of concern, as well as Sage looking at me with the same expression.

"I know, I know, this is scary. This shouldn't have happened," Bailey murmured, rubbing my arms. "You're safe now, sister."

"It's not that." Sniffling, I try to quell the wave of emotion roiling within me.

"What is it then, dear?" Sage asks, her brows furrow.

Elijah has noticed my tears, and has started to move toward me, when all my emotion erupts from me. "I just *really* wanted chocolate chip cookies, and now all the ingredients are *ruined*!" I wail, my breath escaping me in uncontrollable sobs as hormones take control of my bodily functions, causing me to fucking lose my shit in front of my mate, my sister-in-law, and mother-in-law over *fucking chocolate chip cookies.*

There's a beat of silence as everyone takes in the fact that no, I'm not crying because I was almost beaten or kidnapped or whatever the fuck Thallia was about to do to me, but because as a result of this attack, I lost out on my opportunity to make the cookies I've been craving since I thought of them an hour ago.

A laugh bursts from Elijah's chest before he smacks his hand over his mouth, earning him a glare from his mother, which he shrunk away from immediately.

Seeing Elijah get the side eye from his mom, a woman no taller than me, makes my emotions do a 180, making me flip from crying hysterically to releasing a giggle.

Everyone stares in shock at my apparent bipolar disorder, until I'm full out laughing. Elijah catches my eye and grins, his previous chuckle fully letting loose from his chest, which leads to Laurent and Bailey joining in, and even earns a chuckle from Sage.

Once I calm down, I start gathering cleaning supplies from under the sink. "What are you doing?" Elijah demands, his voice lined with disbelief.

"Cleaning up this mess?" Isn't it obvious?

"Oh, no." Sage tuts me, taking the cleaning supplies from me. "You've had enough excitement for one night, you get yourself to bed. Laurent, Bailey, and I will take care of this."

Elijah leads me up the stairs, and the sound of Bailey teasing Laurent for being lumped in with the cleanup crew brings a small smile to my face. Elijah kisses my hair, and walks with me to our room.

"Are you coming to bed tonight?" My voice is hopeful. He's been falling asleep in his office the last couple of nights. I hope nothing too serious is going on.

"Nothing can keep me from you, baby." He smiles at me, and we go to bed, my head resting on his chest, feeling like I finally have a real family.

I'm woken up in the morning by Elijah gently running his fingers through my hair. "Good morning," I murmur sleepily, and he smiles softly at me before his expression goes serious, "What's wrong?" Sitting up, I take his hand in mine.

"I went into my office this morning. It didn't sit well with me that whoever attacked you somehow knew you'd be in the kitchen by yourself...I found this under my desk." He holds up a tiny black button looking thing. "It's a bug," he says, noting my confused expression. "Someone's been listening to me...us. And I can't help but think that Thallia would have had the perfect opportunity to plant it the night you were taken."

This confirms it.

It was Thallia.

"Did they find her last night?" My voice is hoarse.

Shaking his head, he squeezes my hand. "No. Nobody's seen her since yesterday afternoon and she's not answering my mindlink, either. It looks like she made a run for it."

She's gone?

"That's good," I say, rubbing my hand on his arm. "She can't mess with us anymore."

Rubbing his neck, he looks out the glass of my balcony doors. "I don't know, Lu, something about this whole thing feels…unfinished. She's gone for now, but she's still out there. What if she comes back? I let her into our lives, and I—"

He stops when I take his face in my hands. "It is *not* your fault," my voice rings with conviction, "Every poor choice, she made *herself* when you had done nothing but be understanding and give her a chance," Kissing him deeply on the lips, I rest my forehead on his as I continue, "you are a *good person*, Eli. You are not your father. You can't punish people without proof, so don't ever feel bad about that."

"I don't deserve you," he breathes, wrapping me in his arms.

"Nobody does," I tease, and he tackles me to the bed, our laughter eventually drowned out by our fervent kisses.

Chapter 26

Epilogue

Lucy

One week later and there's still no sign of Thallia. I know I should count that as a good thing, but part of me wishes she would just jump out of whatever dark pit she's hiding in so we can take her down once and for all. Despite Elijah's assurances that everyone in the pack knows to detain her on sight, I can't help but jump at every shadow or the knots that appear in my stomach when I hear footsteps when I'm alone. It's always Bailey or Silvy, or one of the warriors coming to check on me.

We're at the Pack Doctor's office, and Elijah bought one of the hospital's ultrasound machines so we don't have to take any risks by traveling to the hospital. He paid to have it towed here on in a *very* padded crate, and Doctor Sullivan had just gotten it hooked up when we showed up for our appointment.

Shivering as the cold jelly makes contact with the ever increasing swell of my belly, Doc moves it around, trying to find the baby as Elijah grasps my hand. A constant whooshing noise fills the room, and I look at the screen in shock. "Is that...?"

"That's the heartbeat," Doctor Sulllivan smiles at us, maneuvering the wand some more, until we see a baby-shaped blob on the screen. "And there is your baby."

Our mouths gape open as we watch the screen, and the baby-shape moves their arms and legs around like they're dancing. "Is it normal for them to be that...active?" Elijah asks, his voice full of awe.

Doctor Sullivan chuckles, as he clicks around the screen, taking measurements of the baby's head and limbs. "Yes, it is quite common. Some babies are more active at different points of the day, and it looks like we hit this one's power hour."

Speechless, I stare at the screen that holds the image of my baby. We created a miracle. We created *life*.

"Do you have a better idea of a due date now?" Elijah asks for me. We went over my list of questions before leaving the pack house, but I didn't plan on being quite so dumbstruck that I couldn't ask my own questions.

"I do." He nods. "Based on her current gestational state of 13 weeks, one day, and the rate the baby is growing, I'd say you'll have a full term baby at about 28 weeks."

"Twenty eight weeks?" I blurt out, my voice finding me again. "That means I'm almost halfway done. You said werewolves have a gestational term of 30 weeks."

"I did. I also said that human-wolf shifter interbreeding is uncertain territory, and it varies from couple to couple depending on many different factors." He isn't rude in his response, just factual.

Nodding, I swallow as I try to take in the fact that in 15 weeks I'll have a baby to hold.

"Do you want to know the gender of the baby?" Doc asks, smiling kindly at us again.

"Isn't it a little early for that?"

"If it was a human pregnancy, you'd have to have a blood test to get the answer. But with your 28 week term, you're at the point in your pregnancy that humans would be in their twentieth week, so we can tell from the ultrasound."

Elijah and I exchange a glance. We had decided that if we could, we would want to know the gender whenever they were able to tell us. I just didn't think it would be so soon.

"We do." Elijah nods, and Doctor Sullivan turns the screen towards him, focusing back on the ultrasound machine, clicking a few more times.

"Ah," he says, turning the screen back towards us. "If you look in this small box, you'll see—"

"It's a boy?" My voice escapes me, my eyes zeroing in on the little tiny boy parts in the ultrasound.

Elijah chuckles as Doctor Sullivan confirms, "Yes, it's a boy."

A boy.

I always wanted a boy first, and then a girl. Smiling, I turn towards Elijah as he plants a kiss on my lips. "We're having a boy." He grins. "An heir for the pack! We have to think of names!"

A laugh escapes me at his enthusiasm, and Doctor Sullivan wipes my belly of the jelly, helping me pull my shirt back over my belly.

"We're all set here," he says, brushing off his pants. "We'll have another check up in about two weeks."

Elijah helps me to my feet, and we thank the doctor, before he catches us. "Oh, one more thing."

Exchanging a confused glance with Elijah, we turn back towards the doctor.

"I don't want to step on any toes..." He looks slightly uncomfortable. "And I hope you don't find this observation disrespectful, Alpha, but I noticed that the mate bond has not been completed yet."

Elijah goes rigid next to me. Now that I think about it, he had stopped mentioning the mate bond altogether after he angrily made that comment about forcing it on me.

This is the first time I've seen this human doctor look even slightly nervous. He can obviously tell this is a touchy subject for Elijah since the look on his face screams *"tread carefully."*

Doctor Sullivan raises his hands in a placating gesture. "All I wanted to say, and again, I know *nothing* about your circumstances. However, *if* the reason you're holding back on completing the mate bond is because of the baby...I just wanted to inform you that it would not hurt the baby."

The tension leaves Elijah's shoulders as he goes into a state of cool indifference. "Thank you for the information."

A sigh of relief escapes the Doctor before we turn and exit the office. Elijah tucks me under his arm as we trek back to the pack house in silence, the new information turning in my head.

"Eli?" He inclines his head toward me in acknowledgment as we continue walking. "Is that why you stopped talking about the claiming?"

Rubbing the back of his neck, he looks towards the sky, "It had crossed my mind."

"Oh."

Do I want him to claim me?

I love him, I'm having his baby, I'm planning on staying in the pack with him...

"Do you mind if I go see Bailey?" I ask innocently, breaking away from his side.

"Yeah, I'll see you later baby. I've got some work to do." He kisses my cheek before I practically skip towards Bailey's house, needing more than one favor if I'm going to pull tonight off.

"Come in," I call, laying across our bed in what I hope is a sexy pose. The candles lining the room cast me in a very flattering glow, and Elijah's eyes darken as he enters the room, taking in the sight of me.

I had gone to Bailey earlier in hopes she knew of where I could acquire some lingerie, and she more than delivered. She claims she ordered it for me weeks ago as a scandalous baby shower present. I'm draped across our bed in a see-through black teddy that has a lace trim. There's a curtain opening right under the bust that puts my baby bump on full display. The g-string it came with is riding up my ass, but it'll be worth it to see Elijah peel it off with his teeth.

"This is a pleasant surprise," he rumbles, moving towards me like a predator. "When Bailey said you wanted to see me upstairs, I definitely wasn't expecting *this*."

"I wanted tonight to be special," I breathe, standing on my knees on the bed, revealing the way his eyes rove my body, his raging hard on pressing against the front of his pants.

"It's always special with you, Lucy." How can he say things like that and not expect me to melt into a blubbering mess?

"But tonight is different." I walk on my knees to the edge of the bed where he meets me, placing his hands on my waist. They don't stay there, though. They run up and down my sides causing goosebumps to erupt all over my body.

I stare at his beautiful, sky blue eyes until the realization dawns on him, his eyes growing wide and his breath hitching in his throat. "You don't mean..."

Biting my lip, I nod. "I want you to complete the mate bond, Elijah. I want you to claim me, and I, you. I love you and am never going to leave."

His mouth crashes into mine as a groan leaves him, and he pushes me back so I'm laying back down on the bed. Lifting himself briefly, his eyes flash as he really takes me in. "You're so fucking beautiful, Lucy." he growls, then launches himself at me. He devours me, nipping, licking and sucking at my lips until I'm breathless.

A soaking mess.

Desperate for him.

"No foreplay." I shake my head, breaking the kiss, when he moves his hand down to my aching center. "I need you, Elijah." Staring desperately into his eyes, I say, "Make me yours."

"As my mate commands," he growls, ripping the thong off of me in one swift movement.

"That was new!" I protest, but my words are quickly swallowed by his mouth on mine, and he captures my moan as he plunges straight into my core, burying himself to hilt.

"Elijah!" I cry holding on for dear life as he drives into me, the fact that he's about to claim me no doubt sends both him and his wolf into a frenzy.

"Lulu," he grunts between thrusts, his face buried in my neck as he works the area where my neck meets my shoulder. "Tell me when you're close."

Each of his thrusts sends me higher and higher on waves of ecstasy, until finally, I can feel it start to break, "I'm co—"

My words are cut off by sharp pain where Elijah's mouth was moments before, causing me to cry out. His teeth are sunk into the tender spot in between my neck and shoulder. The pain, however, dances with my pleasure, causing the wave to soar higher as the burning fades only to be surpassed by the most intense euphoria I've ever experienced. His teeth have left my neck, quickly replaced by his tongue languidly licking the spot of bite, soothing any lingering burn.

As I tumble over the edge, screaming into the void in a way I never have before, a voice enters my mind, *"Mark me, Lucy,"*

Elijah?

I don't know if I'm doing this right, but I lift my head as he continues to thrust into me, and bite as hard as I can into the soft tissue of his neck, the same place he marked me. As my teeth pierce his skin, he moans so loudly I'm sure they'll hear us all the way on the first floor. Quickly removing my teeth, I mimic what he did to me, licking the wound with a flat tongue as he shudders, emptying himself inside of me.

He slows to a stop as we both breath hard, and he rolls off me, his back on the bed, staring at the ceiling as he catches his breath.

"I had known it was going to be that good, I would have let you claim me the first night,"

He turns his head towards me, a silly smile on his face. "You got the hang of mind-linking pretty quickly."

"What can I say? I'm a quick learner." I roll onto my side so I'm facing him.

"Once you're initiated as Luna, you'll be able to mindlink the entire pack."

"And now that you're fully mated, you can be officially initiated as Alpha." Throwing my legs over him, I straddle his waist. "You know…" I run my fingers down the front of his shirt, moving to unbutton each of the buttons. "What they don't know is that the Luna is even more powerful than the Alpha."

"Oh really?" He raises a brow, wiggling his hips, causing a moan to escape me as his growing erection rubs against my naked pussy, "How's that?"

"Well, you're below me right now, aren't you?" Trying to make my voice as nonchalant as possible, I grind my hips down on him.

"You're playing a dangerous game, mate," he whispers, pulling me down to him by neck, a playful glint in his eyes.

"Then play with me," I tease.

"Fuck, I love you so much." His mouth encompasses mine, the world lost to us as we go for round two.

And three.

Fuck, I'm sore.

But it was so worth it.

The next morning, I'm standing by our bedroom window, sipping on some tea. Stupid fucking caffeine limits.

It's for the baby…it's for the baby.

Relaxing against the hard body that presses against me from behind, a sigh of contentment escapes me as Elijah places a gentle kiss on my mate mark. I noticed it was completely healed after round two the night before, and Elijah explained it was a "mate bond thing". His mark had healed as well.

Leaning my head back against his chest, his kisses roam my neck. "What are you thinking about?" he murmurs, nibbling my earlobe.

Sighing, I place my tea on the window sill, and turn around to face him, looping my arms around his neck. "I don't know…" A sigh escapes me, and he chuckles.

"Yes you do," he chides. "Tell me what's wrong."

"I guess…I know it seems like the threat is over, but I can't help but think that Thallia will come back and…I don't know, finish what she started."

His eyes get a determined look to them as he says, "I promise you, Lucy, if she ever shows her face or even a hint of her pops up, we'll take care of it. I'm never going to let anything happen to you again." I sigh against his chest as he pulls me to him, kissing the top of my head.

"I know you won't, Eli." I mindlink, because I can, and I tilt my head up to his in a kiss, willing him to comprehend just how far the depths of my love for him go.

Despite wanting to be completely lost in him, however, I can't shake the feeling that someone is watching from the treeline outside our window.

www.ingramcontent.com/pod-product-compliance
Lightning Source LLC
LaVergne TN
LVHW010318070526
838199LV00065B/5603